To my children's children.

For further information, contact:
Tumblehome, Inc.
201 Newbury St, Suite 201
Boston, MA 02116
http://tumblehomebooks.org/

Library of Congress Control Number 2021943043
ISBN-13 9781943431762
ISBN-10 1943431760

Wylie, Janet
Menace in the Mist - 1st ed

Printed in Taiwan

10 9 8 7 6 5 4 3 2 1

TUMBLEHOME, Inc.

Menace
in the mist

Janet Wylie

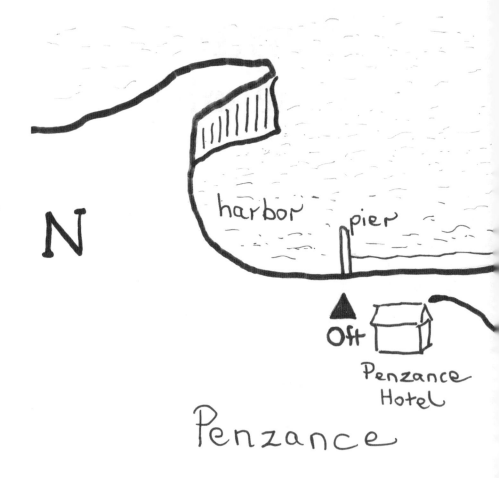

E

ATLANTIC   OCEAN

N

harbor   pier

Off

Penzance
Hotel

Penzance

W

Lighthouse

Foggy
Bottom

80ft

100ft

Moms'
house

quarry

S

Coast Road

120ft

Chapter

1

When her mom said, *A week at the beach,* Cally had imagined sun and sand and sea and ice cream and rock pools and splashing in the waves. She had not thought, *Fog.* Certainly not the dripping kind that makes your hair stick to your head and your skin pucker up with cold.

She leaned over the balcony of their motel room and craned her neck. She had hoped to see the sea, but all she could make out was the dirty white and black number plate on the back of their Subaru Forester. Beyond that, its green body dissolved into grey. There seemed to be no junction between sky and land, as if the parking lot itself was suspended in a thick cloud. The only evidence of their being near the shore was the rhythmic sound of crashing waves echoing through the fog.

"I'm going for a walk," she said, as she opened the sliding door that led back into the motel room. She scanned the room looking for her shoes. Her mother and Aunt

Beth were both stretched out on the matching seashell and sea horse strewn comforters that adorned their queen-sized beds. Seeing them side by side made Cally feel the same pain in her stomach that she'd first felt that terrible summer two years ago, when her mom's cancer was first diagnosed. Their sisterly resemblance was clear, and not just because of the blue jeans and pale t-shirts they both wore. They were dark haired, the same height, with the same long neck. But Janie, Cally's mom, looked skinnier than her sister and still had dark circles under her eyes, two years after her breast cancer treatment. *Stop thinking about it,* she said to herself. She definitely needed a walk.

"Not on your own, you're not." Her mother's predictable response. "Not in this weather."

"Giles, you go with her," Aunt Beth said.

Cally sat down on the floor next to her shoes and glanced over to the corner where her cousin was seated, his head bowed over a screen. He showed no sign of having heard. Giles was on another planet, or so it seemed. During the entire drive to Maine from Vermont the previous day, he had never so much as turned his head to look at her. His long, thin body had remained hunched over his phone, like a magician concocting a spell. Cally knew that if she'd kept her head down like that she'd have been car-sick. So, no, he did not appear to be the walking, or talking type. No way he'd want to go with her to explore the beach. She wondered why he'd even come on this vacation.

Giles was not Cally's real cousin, more of a step-cousin, because Aunt Beth was not Giles' mom. They were step-cousins because Aunt Beth had married Giles' dad earlier in the summer. Giles' dad was her new Uncle Ernest, a pretty unfortunate name for an uncle. Giles was two years older than Cally, already fourteen, and the only thing that she had in common with her ginger-haired step-cousin was that they both had spindly bodies and long legs.

No, that was wrong, Cally thought. They did have something else in common. Something very sad. Both their real moms had had the same disease. They'd both suffered from breast cancer. With one big difference— her mom HAD got better, and his real mom (she didn't even know her name) had died. How awful must that be? No wonder Giles was quiet.

The room suddenly felt too small for Cally. She needed to get out—the moms couldn't stop her. She slid her feet into her sneakers and concentrated on the laces.

"Go on, Giles. You two go and explore," Aunt Beth repeated. "It could be fun."

"Like you'd know," he said, his voice harsh, sarcastic.

Cally couldn't believe it. Why was he so rude to Aunt

Beth? She watched as he uncurled his coiled frame from the seat, grabbed an orange parka, picked up his brick red cell phone and headed for the door. The door slammed shut behind him.

Cally looked over at her aunt in time to see a flush appear on her cheeks. "I guess I said the wrong thing again," Aunt Beth said, as she swung her legs off the bed.

"Don't take it so hard, Sis," said Cally's mom. "He's just being a teenager."

"Tell me about it," Aunt Beth said with a sigh.

Cally decided to make her exit while she had the chance. And anyway, the moms looked like they needed to have a heart to heart on the subject of Giles. She didn't need to witness that.

"I'm going out too," she said. "I mean, I'll go and see if he wants company."

Chapter

2

Outside, Cally looked around and saw only fog. A thick, all-encompassing cloud. Still, better than being cooped up inside, she thought, even if I walk in circles. She wondered which way Giles had gone. She zipped up her hoodie and walked out into the parking lot.

"You escaped too?" A voice to one side of her. She smiled as Giles' orange parka appeared out of the mist.

"Too right," she said. "I need a walk."

"I think the beach is this way," he said pointing to their right. "Follow me."

Cally thought about it. Why not? she decided. At least he hadn't said, *Go away.*

Cally gradually relaxed as she walked, just happy to be out of the claustrophobic atmosphere of the hotel bedroom. Giles strode out ahead, his orange rain jacket a beacon in the fog. She picked up her pace to keep up. Her feet echoed as they scrunched on the sandy footpath that ran alongside the road. Ahead she heard the thrum of waves coming ashore and then sucking back over sand. It told her the shore must be close. So strange not to be able to see beyond the veil of grey. Was the tide out or in? How wide was the shoreline? Was it sandy or rocky or covered in sea-weed? It had been dark and rainy the previous evening when they'd arrived, so they'd not yet had a chance to explore. Her mom's description from the tourist website, *Penzance has a quaint harbor,* was all she had to go on.

The road, empty of traffic, ended abruptly in a parking lot. They climbed over the iron railing surrounding the lot. Condensation on the metal bars wetted Cally's hands and the inside-legs of her jeans as she crossed. She realized that her face was damp with sea-fret. They jumped down and their feet crunched onto pebbles.

"Pretty eerie," said Giles.

"Right," she agreed. They stood still for a while, listening. The fog hung round them like the soaked walls of a tent. Cally still could not see the sea, but its sound raked repeatedly in her ears. They followed the noise out to the water's edge where white-flecked waves hammered out of the mist into the shore. With no visible landmarks to aim for, Cally focused on the foghorn's sound. It was like a herd of cows mooing in sync.

"Let's go this way," she said, pointing along the beach. She was surprised when Giles set off in the suggested direction, apparently anxious to lead the way. She started after him, counting out-loud the interval between blasts. One, two, three… eighteen, nineteen, MOOOOOOOOO. Giles seemed unmoved by her refrain. He walked on ahead as she timed her step with her counts.

They strode along the shoreline, her mooos reverberating back through the fog. Cally noticed how Giles' footprints ahead of her filled with water as soon as his feet left their mark, the sand was so wet. As they walked, the beach was gradually replaced by yellow-grey rocks and rock pools. They advanced with their heads down, leaping across pools and sliding over seaweed-strewn surfaces. The noise of the sea grew louder and the spray higher as they sprang from rock to rock. Cally changed her moos to Wows as she leapt forward, but her voice was drowned out by the waves.

She almost collided with Giles when he stopped suddenly.

"Whoa!" he said.

She looked up. Ahead, the rocks became huge boulders and the cliff face loomed in front of them out of the fog.

"We'd better go back," he said.

They both turned to retrace their steps. Cally was

now in the lead. She jumped over one rock pool and balanced on the next outcrop. She looked to left and right to try to see the way she had come. But the rock she was standing on was now separated from the next by a wide gap, a channel that was too big to leap, a gap that was filled with water. Each roll of the tide brought a further torrent of water along the trench.

Cally stared down at the rushing water. "Hey, what happened?"

Giles caught up with her. "Uh, the tide came in?"

"Right. Well I guess we can't go this way. We need to get closer in to the shore."

Cally turned and went forward again. She knew she should move faster but which way? The tide was encroaching on both sides. She felt Giles hand on her arm and looked back into his wet face. He was staring ahead, biting his bottom lip. His look told her everything. He's as scared as I am, she thought.

"It's too late," he said.

Cally followed his gaze. Grey fog rolled over water. Water behind, crashing; water to their right, rocks being submerged in froth; to their left a row of stone pillars surrounded by sea. In front the cliff face. The wet surface on which they were balanced was fast becoming an island. Cally tried to concentrate on not slipping off. How could the water have come in so quickly? Why hadn't she noticed?

"Now what?" she shouted.

"Guess we'll have to go up." He pointed at the cliff face. "Up there."

Cally stared at the waves crashing against the cliff. The huge, steep cliff. She couldn't even see the top through the fog. It was made up of horizontal layers, black slabs dripping with moisture, interspersed with dark yellow-grey boulders, and out-jutting ledges that protruded at odd angles.

She looked from the cliff to Giles. "That's not even funny."

"We don't really have a choice," he told her.

"Wait... seriously?" She didn't want to seem like a wimp, but climbing a cliff? "Umm, I'm not really a climb-er."

"Well, you're about to become one. Come on." Cally felt herself being tugged forward. Giles' hands were strong. She wanted to dig her heels in, to protest, to get her breath. Why couldn't she breathe?

His face was suddenly right next to hers—serious, stern, his eyes bright with determination.

"Come ON! You've got to. Do what I do. Follow me."

The feeling of cold on her heels, of the sea soaking

her socks, made up her mind. Giles moved. She followed. They ran and splashed over rocks and pebbles and made it to the cliff face. Giles did not hesitate. Cally took a breath. Giles was right. She didn't have a choice.

He started climbing, calling instructions over his shoulder:

"This bit's slippery."

"Take a hold here."

"Grab this branch."

"Rest a minute."

On and on and on. The noise of the waves was lost, blocked out of her brain by her need to follow his instructions. The world became Giles' voice, Giles' feet, Giles' words, her own breath and the fog, the taste of salt, the smell of wet rock and sweat. *Concentrate*, she thought. She had no feel of time, just lungs bursting, muscles tight, shoulder blades aching, jaw locked…

Until,

"Made it!" A holler from above.

And the world turned from vertical to flat as Cally crawled forward on all fours onto solid, horizontal ground. The grass was soaking wet, but she didn't care.

Thank you, she thought. Thank you to Giles, to God if there was one, and to her body for getting her up the cliff.

"Holy crap," she said, breathing hard. "That was intense."

She crawled another foot from the edge of the cliff. Her right hand sank into something sticky and soft. She pulled it back, as if she'd touched an open flame, and looked down.

"Eeewww!" It was so gross. Her fingers were covered in black and white feathers, matted together with dark red-brown goo. Was that blood?

"Disgusting!" she cried and sank back down on the wet ground.

Chapter

3

"What's up?" Giles was at her side. "Come away from the edge." He motioned her forward.

Cally stared at her hand, then at the disgusting mess in front of her. She tried to wipe off her hand on the wet grass but her fingers were still stuck together. The smell of dead animal hit her and she turned her head away.

"I put my hand in something. It's really gross."

She got to her feet, staggered forward and held out her horrible hand.

"Sick," Giles agreed, "but better than dog shit." He picked a feather off her finger. "Definitely dead bird." He looked around and started to tear wet fern fronds from the adjacent rocks. "Try wiping it with this."

She rubbed some of the mess away.

"Oh God. I think it was a seagull," she said. "Maybe there's a puddle somewhere I can wash my hands in?" She looked around.

"Don't worry about it." Giles seemed to have lost interest and was already moving away into the fog. His ginger hair was now dark and plastered flat to his head, ears sticking out like bat wings as he disappeared between wet black rocks and bramble bushes. Behind her the waves crashed against the cliff face. Cally raced to catch up. She did not want to get left alone in this creepy place.

As they trekked forward and upward, the noise of the waves against the cliffs gradually faded. A hundred yards or so further on they were able to speak without shouting.

"There's got to be a road up here somewhere," Giles said. He pulled his phone out of his pocket and wiped the moisture off the screen. "Not much of a signal. Let's keep walking away from the cliff."

The mist continued to swirl around, but the sky looked lighter and brighter to the west, away from the sea. Out of that horizon she saw two birds—ducks maybe—silhouetted, low-flying, skimming the bushes above the mist. They quacked in unison, flew straight across her line of vision and descended over the hillside, out of view. Their quacking faded and was replaced by a distinct *splash*.

"There must be water over there," she said.

Cally ran forward and stopped. Ahead, the land fell away, as if a giant had taken a bite out of a hillside cake.

"Wow," she said.

Giles joined her.

"Awesome," he said.

They stood at the rim of a mist-filled crater, with a dark edge that curved away out of view into the fog. It was impossible to see how wide the crater was, or how far down it went, but the way the quacking and splashing echoed and faded over and over again, in and out of her hearing, suggested that it was a big body of water and that it was a long way down the steep-sided cliffs to the water's edge.

Cally rubbed her eyes and looked again. There was something else. Flashes of white, down and to her right—something weird moving through the mist. Was it a person? An animal?

"What's that?" She pointed in the direction of the movement.

"What?" Giles turned his head, but whatever had been there was gone.

"There was something moving over there."

"I didn't see it. Maybe it was a deer?"

"No. It was white."

"Could have been a deer's tail."

"Maybe." That did make sense, but… there was something else. The creepiness she had sensed before on the cliff top came back to her. "Do you smell that? Something stinks. It's like before, from the dead bird."

Giles didn't answer; his attention was back on his phone.

"Any luck with the signal?" Cally really wanted to get away from this place.

"It's getting better. At least I've got one bar now. Not enough for Google maps though."

"Let's try over there." Cally pointed toward the place she had seen the deer or whatever it was. "Maybe that deer was on a path."

"OK. Maybe a better signal higher up," Giles agreed.

They slipped across grass, weed and pebbles to what did appear to be a deer path. It wound its way uphill away from the rim of the crater. The quacking sound of the ducks faded into the distance behind them. They walked in single file as the mist gradually cleared. Ten minutes further on, the path veered steeply down again. Cally pulled up, out of breath from the climb up to this point, and Giles, in an effort to avoid slamming into her, skidded on the loose soil and gravel, lost his footing and fell on his butt.

"Yow!" he cried. He sat up looking slightly abashed. "Watch it, will you," he muttered.

"Sorry. I just didn't see how the path goes down all of a sudden and…"

He got up and dusted himself off. "It's OK."

They looked around. The ground fell away below them again but this time there was no fog. This looked like a man-made crater. It reminded Cally of a quarry she'd seen in the Green Mountains in Vermont, a quarry that was only visible from a car on the interstate if you happened to look out at just the right moment. And this view had the same effect on her. It was a shock, the shock of a beautiful landscape of trees and hills suddenly scarred, replaced by stark, man-made walls and jagged rocky outcroppings. She looked down into the quarry and saw at the bottom the evidence of discarded industry, a jumbled mass of dirty-orange rusted metal drums interspersed with slabs of grey-green slime-covered concrete like gravestones in an overgrown graveyard. This scene screamed WASTE DUMP.

"That's gross," said Cally.

"Smells bad, too," agreed Giles.

Cally sniffed. "Yeah. Even worse than before."

"And different. Something more chemical than dead bird." Giles lifted his freckled snub nose and mimed sniffing as if he were at a wine tasting. "Hints of gas station, I think," he said in a faux sophisticated voice. "And perhaps a hint of toxic waste."

Cally laughed. This was a new side of him. He was being funny. "Ha. Don't you hate it when adults get all, 'Look at me, I'm such a wine expert.'"

Giles smiled. "Yeah. Especially when it's probably some cheap crap they bought at Costco."

Cally was actually starting to enjoy this. But then the disgusting smell and the sight of the waste dump brought her back. "But seriously, those drums must have got down there somehow," she said. "There's got to be a road leading out of here."

"Good point." Giles examined his phone again. "OK!" He did a fist pump. "A signal!" He swiped a few times and then showed her the screen. "Here we are, here's the cliff and the road's over there." He pointed around the edge of the waste pit, studied the phone again, scrolling down. "And it winds down back to Penzance. Great! 2.1 miles. We just need to find a way from here to the road."

They headed along the edge of the quarry, through the branches of yellow ash and scrubby oak trees and tangles of weeds and ferns, looking for a road.

"I think there's a wall over there," Giles said, pointing through the trees. "Let's go."

Sure enough, after a few more minutes of trampling down weeds, they came to a low stone wall topped with a barbed wire fence. "OK. All we have to do is get over that." Giles took off his windbreaker, scrambled up the wall and draped it over the barbed wire. "I can see the road. Come on."

Cally needed no encouragement. She climbed up beside him, took his hand for balance, lifted one leg and then the other over the rain jacket and jumped down on the other side.

Once over, they saw a tall, diamond-shaped sign attached to the wall and facing out towards the road. It showed a black skull-and-cross-bones on a white background. Just in case the message wasn't clear, the word **Danger!** appeared in bold and black below the skull. And below that a second warning, **Trespassers will be prosecuted to the full extent of the law.**

"Oh well," she said, as Giles joined her, "I guess we're criminals now."

Giles took in the sign and its warning. "How were we to know it was private?" he said. "They need to put a sign over there by the cliffs."

"No way was I going to climb back down that cliff even if I'd seen—"

Beeeee-doop, Beeeee-doop, Beeeee-doop—a piercing, electronic ring made them jump. Giles pulled out his cell phone.

"It's Beth," he said.

"Right," Cally nodded. It sounded strange to hear him call her aunt by her first name. But she was his step-mom, not his mom, she reasoned to herself, so of course that's what he would call her.

Giles glanced at Cally. "I'm not going to tell her about any of this." He nodded towards the *No Trespassing* sign.

"Right," she agreed. "My mom would have a seizure if we told her about the cliff, and trespassing... she'd totally freak out." It felt good to be his co-conspirator.

Giles swiped his phone. "Hi," he said. "Yes, I'm good." He looked towards Cally and rolled his eyes upwards so his forehead creased. "Yes, Cally's here. She's OK. We did a long walk. We'll be back in an hour," he said. He nodded at the phone some more, as he kicked a stone onto the road. "Yes. Yes. OK. Right. We will. Bye." Giles turned off his phone.

Chapter

4

They followed the road back down the hill. Ahead of them the town steamed in the midday sun. Cally felt herself warming in its rays. They walked in silence. He's like me, she thought, he doesn't do chit-chat.

They passed a large white road-side sign showing a fishing boat on blue water. The words *Welcome to Penzance* arched above the scene in navy blue. The sign reminded her of the big question that had occupied her on the drive from Vermont. Why take a holiday now? A vacation in September when everyone else was in school? The answers her mom had given, a chance to get to know Giles, a week of vacation-time that her mom had accumulated and needed to use up, didn't really add up.

Earlier that morning she had pretended to be asleep in the bedroom she shared with her mom and Aunt Beth. She'd listened in to their conversation from her lumpy, turn-down sofa bed and hoped they might give some clues. It was all so strange. Why weren't the dads involved? Was something going on there? After all, her dad seemed to be spending a whole lot of time away. And when he was home there had been lots of tense moments, parents stopping a conversation abruptly when she entered the room. Didn't he like being with them anymore?

"Did Aunt Beth tell you why?" she found herself asking.

"Why what?"

"Why we get to have a vacation now? I mean, a week out of school, just a month after we got back from summer recess?"

"Not really. We don't talk much."

Cally wasn't sure what to say to that. Giles and Aunt Beth seemed to be in a cold war. To her knowledge he'd not said more than *yes* or *no* to his step-mother since the vacation started, except for that rude *'like you'd know'* comment back in the hotel room. She tried a different approach. "Why didn't your dad come?"

"Some stuff about revising a book. Needs perfect silence, I guess."

"Yeah. I get that too sometimes, when my mom and dad work at home. It's even worse when they start talking to each other about science. It's like I'm not there. They've gone deaf to my voice." She knew that Uncle Ernest was a writer, *a published author*, her mom had told her, in a tone of awe, as if he'd won some Olympic gold medal. Both her mom and dad were scientists, molecular biologists, at the university in Burlington. And they were intensely interested in their science. Her dad was the boss of one lab, *a leader in his field,* according to her mom. And her mom was a researcher with a different Professor, Professor Lakewood. Entire conversations at the breakfast table could revolve around genes with insane names like *sonic hedgehog* and *bag of marbles,* in the same way that normal people discuss bacon and eggs. Cally was used to zoning out during such discussions.

"Exactly, except that mine get all excited about book reviews." Giles plunged his hands into the pockets of his windbreaker and kicked a stone down the road.

Cally felt encouraged. Maybe he was open to chatting? "My mom said it was a good chance for me to get to know you," she said. She glanced sideways at him. "Not sure she had climbing up cliffs and trespassing on dangerous waste dumps in mind though."

She was rewarded with the flash of a grin on Giles' face. *Wow,* she thought, in triumph. She liked making him smile.

"I got the idea it's supposed to be a chance for me to *bond*"—he made quotation marks in the air—"with Beth," Giles said. "Fat chance of that."

"Right," said Cally. This felt a bit awkward, so she hurried on. "My dad's away at a meeting, in Singapore. Anyway, I still think it's strange. Not that I'm complaining. I'm really, really psyched to have a week out of that place. My mom had to go into the principal's office to explain. Didn't your school kick up a stink?" she said.

"Nah. They're cool, just as long as I do all the homework they've given me. So, what's wrong with yours?"

"Nothing. Everything." Cally sighed. She wasn't going to get into all the ways in which school was a problem for her. It felt too much like being a whiny kid. She'd stick to the mystery of the unexpected vacation for now. "I still don't get why we couldn't have taken the vacation in the..."

The noise of a dog barking made her stop talking mid-sentence. This was no woof-woof, friendly sound, but a string of high-pitched attack barks, and it was getting louder and louder. A large, black and white collie rounded the corner and headed straight towards them, its fur spread out like ragged sails. It did not slow as it drew close, but nor did it attack. Instead it circled behind them, mouth agape, saliva flowing. They stopped dead in their tracks.

"Whoa, fella," Giles said.

"Wow, you're excited." Cally put her hand out. Maybe

if the dog could sniff her, he'd calm down, she thought. But no, he wasn't interested in sniffing. After another volley of harsh barks, he fixed his eyes on Giles and started to nip at the leg of his jeans, spittle oozing from his mouth. He got a mouth full of cotton and pulled, front legs raised off the ground.

"Get off me!" Giles tried to shake free.

Cally attempted to get hold of his brown collar, but the dog kept moving his head from side to side, yanking Giles forwards with each pull.

"Get the hell off!" Giles shouted again.

"Down dog, down." Cally made another unsuccessful grab at the dog's collar. He barked louder. She glanced down the road. Where was his owner? Why was he so upset?

The collie seemed to notice the change in her attention. He stopped pulling on Giles, stared hard at Cally and whined. He too looked down the road and then turned his head back to her and yapped. The yapping and the stare reminded Cally of something.

"I get it," she said. She'd remembered Bonnie, her neighbor's dog back home. He would always look hard at a stick you were holding and yap at you when he wanted you to throw it for him. This dog wasn't trying to hurt Giles or her, she thought, he wanted them to go with him.

"I think he wants us to follow him," she said. At that instant, the collie loped off as far as the corner. He stopped, turned and barked at them.

"You're right," Giles said. "Let's go." They ran.

The dog raced ahead, but each time he reached a corner in the road he stopped abruptly, turned and barked again. As soon as they caught up, he set off again. Cally wondered if the collie thought they were sheep, and was busy practicing his herding instincts. If so, he was succeeding. She was making her best speed but Giles was still in front. She caught up to him in time to see the collie turn right down a dirt road lined on either side by tall pines. The dog then turned a corner out of sight. They followed him round the bend and stopped. At the end of the drive stood a cedar-clad Cape cottage. The dog had jumped onto the front porch and was turned to look at them, barking up a storm. But there were no welcoming human cries or angry shouts of *Quit that noise* from the dog's owner.

"Come on," said Cally, as Giles hesitated.

"This is definitely trespassing," he said.

The dog leapt off the porch, bounded five paces towards them, then turned back towards the deck.

"But he wants us to come." Cally ran down the path. By now the dog was balancing on his back legs scratching at the fly screen on the front door. Cally realized the door itself was open. Anyone inside could surely hear the noise.

"Hello," Cally shouted. "Is anyone there?"

Giles came up beside her. The dog renewed its efforts to get through the screen.

"There's got to be someone inside," she said.

"Let's find out," Giles pushed the catch on the screen, and it opened outwards towards him. The collie leapt forward and disappeared inside. The barks were replaced by a sad, yipping cry. They found the dog crouched on the stone floor of the kitchen.

The body that lay there was flat on its back, motionless. Cally ran forward and realized she was looking at an old lady, face upward, eyes closed, arms out like a snow angel. But not wrinkled old. Her face was strangely smooth and palest pale, like a full moon surrounded by a cloudy halo of curly grey hair. She was shorter than Cally, but at least twice as wide, and was dressed in an incongruous polka-dotted pink shirt and very old, very baggy jeans.

Maybe she's just sleeping, was Cally's first thought. But the paleness of her face and the sad, yipping cry of the collie gave the lie to that idea. This was clearly the dog's owner. She did not move. Was she unconscious or dead?

"Call 911," Cally gasped.

Giles already had his phone out.

Cally tried to remember the training they'd had in 6th grade. *Don't move the injured person. Take their pulse.*

"Ambulance," she heard him say into the phone. She reached out for the lady's wrist. Could she feel a pulse? Her own heart was pounding in her head. She tried to locate the right spot on the wrist. The old lady's skin felt warm. Was that her pulse or was she feeling the blood pulsing through her own hand? Cally couldn't be sure.

"Old lady. Looks like she's fallen. She's unconscious." There was a pause and then Giles' voice again, impatient. "I don't know the address. It's a cottage next to the coast road south of the town."

"The first turn-off in town down the hill after the *Welcome to Penzance* sign," Cally added.

Giles repeated that information, listened and nodded. "OK," he said and turned off his phone. "They said just to wait. Not to do anything. To stay with her."

So that was what they did. Cally knelt on one side with the dog and Giles on the other.

"I think she's breathing. Do you?" she ventured, after they'd sat for a few moments.

"Yeah. Definitely," said Giles. "Hello, there," he said more loudly. Still no movement, no answer, except from the dog.

Cally felt like she was watching a movie. She stroked

the dog's coat, finding comfort in his warm, soft fur. He kept up his low yip, but did not pull away or try to touch his owner. One smart dog, she thought. "Hang on, collie's mom," she said to the supine form. "The ambulance is coming."

Something smells really off in here, she thought. She sniffed the dog, but he smelled just doggy. Then it came to her. It was the same smell as the one at the dump. The one they'd laughed about.

"Can you smell that?" she asked Giles.

"What?"

"The bad smell. It's like the dump."

Giles took a long breath in, and made a face. "You're right." He got up and headed towards the sink, sniffing like a beagle. "And it's really bad over here."

The dog heard the sirens first. He bounded up and raced to the front door. Giles ran after him, opened the door and waved. The noise of the emergency vehicle rose to a crescendo, then a screech of brakes and the sound of voices. Before she knew it, Cally felt herself being hauled up by the armpits and guided outside.

"You've done everything you can now miss," the uniformed first responder said. The woman's dark face was kind as she patted Cally's shoulder and then hurried back inside the house. A second younger man was rolling a gurney out of the ambulance past them into the house.

"You did a good job calling this in," he said as he passed by. "Good thing you weren't in school."

"We don't live here," Giles started to explain.

"Tell Officer Whistler," he said as the screen door shut behind him.

Cally and Giles turned to see a policeman climbing out of a police car next to the ambulance. The officer was grim-faced with a slight swing to his gait. He had crew-cut hair, a gun on his hip, eyes hidden by dark sunglasses even though the sun was behind a cloud, and a notebook in hand. He was not the friendly face of law enforcement that Cally was used to seeing at school. The questions came thick and fast:

"OK. Names and ages?"

"Giles Sherman, fourteen."

"I'm Cally, short for Pascale, Mountbatten. I'm twelve."

"What's your relationship to the lady?"

"None," said Giles.

"We don't know her," added Cally.

"So how did you come to find her?"

They explained about their vacation and how the dog had led them to her. Cally could not make out the expression behind the sunglasses. Officer Whistler continued to write as he spoke.

"So, you didn't see her fall?"

"No," they said together.

The officer looked up from his notebook. He put his pen behind his ear, pushed the sunglasses off his nose onto his forehead, and the grim face was transformed by a dimpled smile. "Well done, you two."

Cally took a deep breath. *Phew*, she thought.

"What about the dog?" she asked. The poor collie had been tied to one of the uprights on the deck. He'd had to watch his mistress wheeled away out of the yard. The ambulance was gone as quickly as it had appeared. His barking decreased to a whimper as the sound of the siren died away.

"Animal services will take care of him for now. He'll be fine. OK, you two can head back to your hotel. Thanks for calling this in. Do you want a ride?"

Cally looked at Giles. He looked down at his phone.

"It's two o'clock," he said. "They're gonna be mad."

"Yes, we'd love a ride," Cally told the policeman.

Chapter

5

Cally saw her mom and aunt in the lobby of the hotel when they climbed out of the police cruiser. Her mom caught sight of them before Aunt Beth. She was wide-eyed and rigid as she met them at the swing-door. The police car was already gone.

"What's happened?" she said. She looked out of the door, as if to check whether she'd really seen a police car. "Are you OK?"

"We were worried about you," said Aunt Beth, coming up alongside her sister.

Her mom took Cally by the shoulders and looked her up and down. Her grip felt hard. Then she turned her gaze to Giles. He strode past, ducked away from Beth and headed across the lobby.

"Going to the bathroom," he said.

Cally felt all eyes on her. Were they worried she'd

done something really bad? she wondered. "Nothing's wrong," she said hastily. "I'm sorry we're late."

She launched into a description of how they'd followed the dog and found the unconscious old lady. She carefully avoided any mention of climbs up cliffs or trespassing on private land. The adults' faces turned from serious to concerned to smiling by the time she'd finished.

"So, you've no idea what happened to the old lady? Do you think she tripped over something?" her mom asked.

"I don't think so. I didn't see anything around like that."

"Me neither," said Giles as he rejoined the conversation. "Anyway, she'll be in hospital by now. Did you have lunch already? I'm starving."

"Yes, we got tired of waiting for you." Cally's aunt held up a brown paper bag. "We found a great bagel place on Main Street. Here's yours. A BLT for you, Giles…"

"Thanks." Giles took the bag and dove in.

"And smoked salmon and cream cheese for you," said Cally's mom.

Giles extracted Cally's sandwich from the bag and held it out to her.

"Yum. Thanks," said Cally.

"Let's go and sit at that table outside. The sun's really warm," said her mom. "And I need to have a chat with you, Cally, while you're eating." She didn't sound cross, just all business.

"What about?" asked Cally, but her mom was already heading through the revolving door.

"And I'm going to call your dad," said Aunt Beth to Giles, hanging back. "Do you want to come and have a word with him too?"

"OK, I guess," said Giles with a shrug. He seemed more interested in his bagel than in talking to his father, but he turned to follow her upstairs.

Cally felt uneasy, like being in the dentist's waiting room. This whole chat situation seemed a little bit staged. What was it all working up to? She followed her mother outside.

They sat down opposite each other on rickety chairs at the circular metal patio table that radiated white in the afternoon sun. The umbrella and its metal pole had been removed for the Fall season, so the table was warm to the touch. She had taken only one bite of her bagel when her mother began.

"So, you know that one reason for this vacation is for you to get a chance to spend some time with Beth and Giles?" Her tone was serious, her mom's *this-is-important* voice, the voice normally reserved for things like sex education or menstruation. She fiddled with the silk scarf she wore around her neck, the scarf that hid the wrinkles that appeared after her battle with breast cancer.

"Yes."

"So, how's it going? How are you and Giles getting along?"

"Fine. He's quiet, but not in a bad way." Cally felt herself smiling. "He was great over the dog and the old lady. He phoned for the ambulance and everything."

"That's amazing. I can't believe you both did that." Her mom shifted in her seat, as if her thought-train has momentarily been diverted. She took a deep breath. "Anyway, Beth's pretty worried about him. He's angry around her most of the time. She thinks if he gets to know you and me better he'll feel more like part of the family."

Cally nodded. It was clear that Giles had little time for Aunt Beth.

"Why's he so angry with Aunt Beth?" she asked.

"She's not sure. But maybe he resents her because he misses his own mom so much."

"Right." That seemed reasonable to Cally. How would she have liked it if her dad had gone off with someone else, if her mom had died from breast cancer? She put her bagel down. Her interest in eating had faded. A seagull landed on the ground next to them, and it fixed its beady yellow eye on her sandwich.

"So, anyway, there's another reason for this vacation."

"What?" OK, she thought, I knew it. She wrapped up

the rest of the bagel and hid it in her lap. The bird turned away.

"Well, you know Dad's trip to Singapore?"

"Yes." Of course she knew. It was his third trip there this year. And it was definitely causing some strain between her parents that they'd wanted to keep secret. She could tell from the cut-off conversations. She stared past her mom and gripped the sides of the seat. Was that why they were here in Penzance with Aunt Beth? Was he going to leave them?

"It turns out that he's been invited to spend a whole year there, on sabbatical. It's a very prestigious offer."

Prestigious, thought Cally. Who'd ever use that word? At least her Mom hadn't said *he's not coming back.*

"Great," she breathed. She hoped she sounded sarcastic. "What about us?"

"So, the thing is they'll pay for the three of us to live there, in Singapore, for a whole year. After Christmas."

For the first time in the conversation, Cally squinted in the sun to really look at her mom. Her face was in the shade, but her eyes glinted with excitement. She was smiling, bubbly, like a kid about to open Christmas presents.

"To Singapore?"

"Yes. I can work there too, doing my experiments in your dad's lab just for the year, so that's not a problem.

And you can go to school, American school, in Singapore for a year."

"Wow…." Cally paused, trying to take this in. "But why the vacation now?"

"Right. Well, why we're here with Beth and Giles, and what I want you to think about this week is this. If you didn't want to go to school in Singapore, there's another option. You could go and stay with Beth in Albany for the year, and go to the same charter school as Giles."

"What?" This just got weirder and weirder. Why ever would she NOT go with them to Singapore?

Her mom hurried on. "Yes, it's called Albany Stateside Charter for Science and Math. They call it SAM; it's one of the best schools in New York State." She took a deep breath in, sighed it out and patted Cally's leg. "It's your decision. After all the issues at school here, I want you to decide. It should be your decision, not mine and Dad's."

"Wow," she said again. She'd had no idea. What a bombshell. But for sure better than being told that her Mom and Dad were breaking up. "So, have I got this straight?" she said. "I go back to normal school after this week, but then after Christmas I go to Singapore. Or to Giles' school, SAM, right?"

"Right. I know Cloverdale hasn't been fun for you. So, whatever happens, this will be a change. You'd do great either in Singapore or in Albany."

Her mom was right. 6th grade had been terrible. Last year Cloverdale had become an arts magnet school, and it became the school from hell. The sadness started when Emma, her best friend since kindergarten, had moved away. Bishops Stortford was only sixty miles away, and she still saw Emma sometimes, but it was clear that things were different. Emma had made a new circle of friends. So Cally was stuck in Cloverdale with its new emphasis on *Arts*. Then she'd discovered that her favorite math teacher, Mrs. Broomfield, who had let her work on seventh grade math when she was still in sixth, was also leaving. But the worst blow was the crowd of new kids, the ones who'd come because it was an arts magnet school. They all seemed to know each other, shared stories about their ballet and drama performances and talked endlessly about boys. What do you say in answer to their most pressing queries, *Do you like Ryan or Jason? Don't you think Saul's like, super-cute?* Cally blushed at the memory of herself smiling and nodding and thinking *please let the ground open up and swallow me whole.* Sixth grade didn't bear remembering.

So, no, Cloverdale was not working for her. But why spring this on her now?

"Why didn't you tell me before? Before we came?"

"I know, maybe that was a bit silly. But we thought that you don't know Giles very well. So, we talked it over with Beth and she suggested the vacation idea."

"You mean this vacation is a trial?" Cally couldn't help the flash of anger. I mean, honestly? she thought.

"Sort of. But you seem to be getting on well?"

Her mother hadn't even noticed her irritation. She just seemed really, really earnest. Cally relaxed a little.

"Sure. He's OK." She thought about his guiding her up the cliff. And about how he could be pretty funny. "Actually, pretty awesome, when he wants."

"Beth will be pleased to hear that."

"Right. I don't know why he's so mean to her. I mean, she's great. I was fine staying with her when you were sick. But why would I want to go to his school? What's wrong with school in Singapore?"

Her Mom considered that for a moment. "It's an international school. Kids from England and Australia and the US as well as Asia. And that's all great. But it's not a specialist place. Giles' school concentrates on sciences and math. Great teachers. Kids are put in classes depending on ability, not age."

"OK, but if I went to Albany, I wouldn't get to see you and Dad for a whole year, right?"

"No, we'd come back often to see you, and you'll spend all of the summer vacation in Singapore, whatever you decide."

Her mom reached her hand over the table and covered Cally's interlocked fingers.

"Oh sweetie, I was really against the whole idea of you staying here in the US at all. But I do think we should give you the choice. Mrs. Broomfield told me that you should be in an accelerated math program. And you're not getting that at Cloverdale. You'd get it at Albany."

Cally let her fingers relax under her mother's touch. Her mom had at least got that right. But to stay in Albany to get better math lessons? Did that make any sense?

"So, I get to decide?" she said.

"Yes, you do. You're old enough. I'll give you the websites of the two schools. Think about it this week. Chat with Giles about his school. Beth would be over the moon if you stayed with her, she told me so. The deadline to register you for next year in Singapore is coming up soon. Albany Stateside is a private school. I checked and they'd be happy to have you for a year." Her mom sat back in the seat, as if exhausted.

"What about Giles?"

"What do you mean?"

"Is he OK with this?"

"Beth is chatting to him about it now. You can ask him yourself later. How's about a mother-daughter hour on the beach first?"

Cally nodded. She felt lighter. This was a total shock, but it gave her a thrill too. It sounded like life was suddenly going to become much, MUCH more interesting than the weekly grind at Cloverdale Middle School. "Soon as I've finished this," she said. She unwrapped her bagel and took another bite. "It's delicious."

Chapter

6

That evening Cally stood outside Giles' room, hand raised, ready to knock. She knew that Giles would be luxuriating inside, in solitary pleasure. After all, he had his own private room in the hotel, while she had to share with the moms. It was an annoying situation and her mother's pathetic explanation, *he's a boy*, did not help. Even so, she did want to talk about the morning's adventures with Giles, whether or not he wanted to talk about schools.

Suddenly the door flew open.

"I'm going back," Giles announced.

"What?" Cally gasped. "Where?"

He motioned for her to come in. "I'm going back to the quarry."

"Now?" Cally said, confused. Surely, he wasn't planning to go in the dark?

"No, dumb-ass. First thing tomorrow."

Cally felt her face redden. "OK," she said more slowly. "Why?"

"I left my jacket. I just realized. It's draped over that barbed wire fence."

"Right." Cally nodded, as she thought back to the morning. "You're right. I totally forgot about it too. It was just when your mom called." She felt an excited pulse of anticipation. "I'll come too. Let's walk back up the cliff road tomorrow."

"Nah, no need. I'll go early and be back before Beth knows I've gone."

"OK." Cally tried hard to hide her disappointment. It did make sense, she supposed, not to arouse the parents' curiosity.

Giles sat down on a tiny painted wooden chair that creaked its resistance. His knees came up almost to his chest and he still wore the dark, dog-spittle coated jeans he'd had on during the day's outing.

"I bet Beth wouldn't notice," he said. "But it was a present from my dad…." Giles' explanation tailed off.

Cally thought he sounded embarrassed. He'd turned his attention back to the screen that was perched on the matching painted desk. The desk looked like it came from a kindergarten classroom. She decided to change the subject.

"Cool desk," she said, "for a preschooler."

"Right." Giles agreed. She saw the glint of fun in his eyes. "It's got a cool wobble too." He demonstrated by moving his elbow up and down. The laptop jumped.

"Great," she said. "Anyway, I was going to ask, do you want to hang out now?" She shrugged her shoulder to indicate the laptop she was carrying under her arm, just in case he thought he'd have to actually chat with her.

"Sure. You gonna research Singapore?"

"Right. Did Aunt Beth tell you about it? Can you believe it?"

"Yeah, some crazy idea of you coming to Albany instead. Don't do it. Singapore would be so cool."

"You think? I'm gonna google it."

"OK. I've got some stuff I'm doing. And, since you like the desk so much..." He picked up his laptop and stretched out against the headboard of his bed... "You can sit there."

Cally laughed. She'd walked right into that one, she thought.

The bed was almost as funny. Cally noted the rockets and space ships displayed on the comforter. "Fine by me. That comforter is clearly just made for you. I'm happy here."

She took up her appointed station on the chair, opened her laptop and keyed in the website for Singapore American Academy. The home page looked promising, the initials SAA wound around with palm leaves and orchids, against a red backdrop. The embedded video made her eyes widen. The campus looked like an Olympic village, completely new, low buildings set among hillsides covered in banana palms and ferns and lush vegetation, with an outdoor swimming pool and a running track. Kids of all nationalities and all ages. The inside shots showed students making videos, kids doing experiments, acting in a play and playing instruments in an orchestra. All of them were dressed in white shirts and red skirts or shorts, and everyone was smiling.

"Wow," she said.

Giles came off the bed and looked over her shoulder. "Pretty cool."

"But does it look real to you? Can you imagine wearing that gear?"

"Why not? It's boiling hot all the time in Singapore. You'd die in jeans and sweats." He flopped back on the bed.

"So, does your school have a uniform?"

"No way. You wouldn't catch me in red shorts."

"Exactly. They look like a team of Olympic athletes."

"It's got to be better than freezing your butt off doing cross-country in November in New York State."

"Is that what you do?"

"Yeah. You can freeze your butt off at hockey or soccer

but one way or another, you're out there."

"That's cool."

"What, you like workouts? Even with the geeks?"

"What d'you mean?"

Giles rolled over onto his chest, and supported his chin on his hands. "Some of the kids at SAM are seriously geniuses, like budding Einsteins and Marie Curies. I guess that's why they come to SAM, cos they get to study math and science every day. And that means they're not exactly sporty. But we all get to do an hour's workout every day too."

"I wouldn't mind." Cally didn't want to let on that she actually loved the idea of being around other people who loved math and got to run every day. It might be unusual to most people, but those were her favorite things to do. She could add chess to the list, but it wasn't always possible to find people to play.

"Right. Except when the temperature's hovering around freezing and you've got a never-ending cross-country to finish." He put his head down, as if exhausted at the thought.

"OK. I get that." Cally was trying to open the website for Giles' school, but nothing was happening. She clicked again on the site. "Tell me some more."

"Have a look for yourself," he muttered into the comforter.

"I'm trying to. You'd think a school that's full of geniuses would be able to design a website you could open."

"Fair point. Chalk up one plus in the Singapore column?" Giles sat up on one elbow and mimed chalking a mark in the air.

"I guess," Cally said. She gave up on opening the Albany website and turned back to the Singapore one. How good was their math program? The website really was pretty impressive. She found the Middle School drop-down menu and a sample schedule. Monday, Mathematics 12.02 – 1.25pm and again on Thursday for another hour and a half. English appeared every day, but at least there seemed to be no compulsory art or drama or choir, the stuff she dreaded at Cloverdale. That all seemed to be elective. Definitely a plus for Singapore. She closed her laptop with a snap. Giles didn't seem at all interested in persuading her to go to Albany. She sighed, but he took no notice. He was back against his headboard totally focused on his screen.

"What are you looking at?" she said.

"Homework," he said.

"Yuck."

"Right. But I've got an idea," said Giles.

"Yeah?"

"Yeah. So, it's a science project. I have to write about

how stuff's poisoning the environment. Here, listen." He began to read off the screen. *"First, describe a specific pollution problem, second, what is being done to address this problem and third, what else could be done. 1000-1500 word total; 3-5 pages.* Guess what comes to mind?"

Cally knew exactly what he was thinking about. "The quarry, those rusting drums?"

"And that smell…"

"Which one? The dead bird? The dump?"

"Totally. Both. I wish I'd got some pictures, but…"

"You're going back tomorrow anyway," she said.

"Right. But this'll take some time. Beth will wonder what I'm up to." Giles seemed to consider his options.

Cally was already there. "But if I were to come too, they'll just be happy we're *getting to know* each other." Cally made air quotes.

"Good point." Giles nodded. "We'll be *bonding.*" More air quotes.

They both laughed.

"So, you're up for this then? Tomorrow morning?" he asked.

"Sure. Maybe we could borrow the hotel bikes. I saw an ad for them on the front desk."

Cally saw a smile light up Giles' face and crease the corners of his green eyes. When Giles smiles, she thought, he really looks pretty cute….

Chapter

7

The quarry with the skull and crossbones sign was only two miles out of town, but the previous day's journey had been mostly in the police car, so Cally hadn't noticed the hills. In fact, it was mostly uphill. This was the third one she was climbing. Giles was ahead of her, standing up on his pedals, his bike zig-zagging over the crest.

They had just passed the point where the dirt path veered off down to the old lady's house, so she knew there couldn't be much further to go. The hotel's bikes had sit-up-and-beg handle bars and baskets on the front, designed more for picnics than hill-climbs. Cally was beginning to wonder whether they might have been better off walking. The guy on reception had been hard enough to work with. He'd turned out to be Canadian, French Canadian, a man with a pony tail who was determined that they needed to know the French word for bicycle in order to secure the bikes. Turned out it was *vélo* not *bicyclette*. Who'd ever have known that? Anyway, at least the hotel provided lunch supplies. The baskets contained ham sandwiches, snack bars, apples and water bottles, and she was starved. Their moms had been quite content to see them go off for a picnic together, not that they'd told them any details about their plan.

"Keep going," Giles shouted. "I can see the sign ahead." He was astride his bike, leaning over the handlebars. She pedaled harder, in one final effort. Her bike tilted too far to one side, and she lost her balance.

"Whoa!" she said. She got her foot down just in time. She pushed her bike up the last few yards, gasping like a goldfish out of water. Now I know why gears were invented, she thought as she came up alongside Giles.

"Did you find your coat?" she asked. He'd already propped his bike up against the stone wall next to the sign.

"Yep." Giles pointed. "See, it's just where we left it."

Sure enough, she could see a dangling zip and a flash of orange on the top of the barbed wire fence, hanging above the stone wall.

"Do you have the water?" Giles asked.

"Here," she said reaching into the basket.

"Lifesaver," he said.

Cally let her bike drop to the grass at the edge of the

road, took the other water bottle and drank. Water had never tasted so good. She turned around to look back towards Penzance. The view behind was pretty spectacular. Green hills were dotted with late summer yellow grasses and reddening sumac bushes. The hills roller-coasted down to the ocean, where the painted houses of Penzance Point nestled in an inlet. Black fishing boats and white sailboats broke up the blue of the harbor. Ahead of them the TRESPASSERS WILL BE PROSECUTED sign provided a less welcoming picture.

"OK, are we going to do this?" Giles asked.

"Let's eat first." Breakfast really did seem a long time ago.

They settled down with their backs propped up against the wall and ate in silence. The road was very quiet. Cally could count on one hand the number of vehicles that had passed them during their ride.

Giles was the first to finish his sandwich. "So, have you decided?" he asked as he threw the rolled-up paper from his lunch towards his bike's basket. It landed inside.

"Good shot," she said. "About Singapore you mean?"

"Yeah."

Cally shrugged. "I'm still thinking. It actually kept me awake last night." One question had been uppermost in her mind, one she really needed to ask Giles. Now was as good a time as any, she thought. "I wanted to ask you," she began and then hurried on. "Would YOU mind? I mean, would it be weird if I stayed at your house?"

Giles turned and looked at her, a serious look. "It's not my house."

"Well, you know what I mean." She felt her face redden but stumbled on. "Like, I stayed with Aunt Beth a couple of summers back before she and your dad got married." Cally hesitated. She didn't want to mention how she'd stayed with Aunt Beth that whole summer vacation while her mother underwent breast surgery and then chemo and radiation treatments, treatments that had made her mom better. "So I know her house, but it's kinda different now you live there."

"Too right." He said it with a harsh laugh.

"Didn't you want to move in with Aunt Beth?" Maybe that wasn't the right thing to ask, but...

"Not much. We were doing fine in our old place." Giles was picking up pebbles from the ground around him and aiming them at the bike's basket.

"Right."

"But Dad said we needed to move on." He paused and hurled a bigger stone. "HE needed to move on, more like."

"I'm sorry," she said. But before she could get back on to a safer topic, Giles turned.

"It's not your problem. Look, the house is big enough. Too big, really."

"You're sure?"

"Yeah. Loads of space. I only see them at meal-times. You could help field all the questions. You know, *How was your day? What did you learn today?* Constant interrogations." He shrugged. "But you'd have way more fun in Singapore."

"I guess," Cally agreed. Still, she felt a pang of what? Sadness? Rejection?

"If it was my choice," Giles went on, "I'd opt for Singapore." He was getting to his feet.

"Why?"

"Duhh. It's a no-brainer. Adventure. Different everything—climate, people, real jungle, the animals and birds are different. It's got to be way cooler than Albany."

"Right." It was hard to argue with that. Cally hadn't known Giles was interested in those things. She knew that she was more interested in math, honest truth.

"All right, let's do this," He took his small back pack, an incongruous bright green thing with a drawstring top, out of his basket and stuffed the water bottles into it. He put the bag on his back.

"OK, I'm ready." Cally needed no persuasion. She'd gotten her answer.

Giles led the way. The stones in the wall jutted out

enough to make the climb up an easy one, and he used the danger sign to help with balance at the top. He dropped his backpack over and then, "One small leap for man…" he said and disappeared from view.

She laughed, relieved that he was back to making jokes.

"Umphh," was his cry as he landed with a thud.

Cally was about to follow when it occurred to her that leaving the bikes by a NO TRESPASSING sign might not be a good idea. "Wait a minute," she shouted and then pushed her bike along the road a little way until she could prop it up behind a tree, out of sight of the road. She went back for Giles' bike and did the same thing.

"What's the problem?" Giles shouted.

"Nothing, just moving the bikes away from the road."

Cally climbed easily up the stone wall.

"Just jump," he said. "We'll get my jacket on the way back." He was standing in a thicket of brush and bindweed.

"Here I come," she shouted. She landed next to him and he caught her arm to steady her. "Thanks," she said.

"OK," he said. "Step 1 achieved. Let's go to the quarry with the disgusting smell first. I want to take some pictures of those drums."

"And I want to know what's in them. Do you think they're the reason for that sign?"

"Maybe. They're definitely toxic. We should have thought to bring some gloves."

"Too late now. Do you remember the way?" Cally scanned the undergrowth.

"We must have flattened our way through the weeds here somewhere, yesterday," Giles said.

Sure enough, a trampled area of weeds led them to the overgrown path. A few hundred yards along, Cally sniffed the bad smell. It was like inhaling next to a gas pump when her dad was filling the car, sickly sweet but with hints of burnt eggs. The previous Easter she'd been in charge of hard-boiling the eggs in preparation for painting them. She'd become engrossed in something else and totally forgot about them. By the time she remembered, the stove and the ceiling were spattered with yellow flecks of dried egg and brown egg-shell. And the smell… It was that very odor that had jolted her memory and driven her back to the kitchen.

When they reached the edge of the quarry they stopped to find the best route down. Giles led the way towards what seemed to be the least steep part of the slope. As she followed him down, Cally wondered if this was how the rusty oil drums had first been dumped. Had someone rolled them down here? When she made it to the bottom, her feet sank into marshy ground.

Giles let out a long whistle. "Can you believe this?" he said.

Cally took in the scene. It was staggering. From above, most of the drums had been hidden by bushes and over-hanging rocks, but from this vantage point, she saw that they filled almost the whole space. Against the back-drop of the white quarry walls, they made a grotesque piece of abstract art. Each drum stood out, at least half her height and as wide as her body, ridged and rusted in bands of dark grey and burnt orange, streaked with shiny black marks, dented in some cases, swollen in others, some resting on their sides against slabs of crumbling concrete, metal rims breaking off, others piled over each other and surrounded by thickets of grasses and weeds. The closest corroded specimen was caked in blue-black oil. An oily sludge snaked from its underside.

"Gross," she said. She reached down and touched the dark rivulet. She rubbed her fingers together. The oil spread as a thin, slick film. She looked down to see that her sneakers had developed a greasy rim where their surfaces touched the mud.

"This one's definitely leaking oil."

Giles was already taking pictures. "But these have got something different," he said. He was standing by a stack of four or five smaller, fatter barrels. "See, they're all swelled up and the ground here stinks."

Cally looked. The ground around Giles was dead.
Dead grass, brown thorn bush, and a pool of grey water.

"What do you want me to do?" she asked.

"Can you count how many drums you can see?" he
said.

"Sure."

Cally moved around the dump, counting out loud.
She noticed the ground sloped away from her and the
water gathered to a point where it formed a more con-
spicuous stream. Twenty-five, twenty-six… had she already counted that one? She stopped and turned back to
Giles.

"I've counted twenty-five of them, maybe twenty-six.
And that's not counting the small ones. And lots of them
are leaking." The land sloped away to one side where the
rivulets converged. Cally realized there was a stream
running through, lined on either side by goldenrod. It
disappeared into the bushes in front of her.

"I'm going to follow the stream, see where it goes,"
she said.

"OK. Wait for me."

Giles came up beside her. He stowed his phone in the
green backpack and then jumped over to the other side
of the stream. "You go down on your side and I'll try this
way."

They scrambled along in parallel with each other, over fallen branches and around low scrub until they arrived at the cliff and the answer to their question. The water picked up speed as it vanished from view into a dark red, circular pipe. The pipe disappeared off through the hillside.

"Did you get pictures of all the stuff in the water?" she asked. "It's got to be a good example of pollution for your project."

"Some. But I still need a close-up view." Giles dug in his backpack and pulled out one of the water bottles. He poured out the remaining water, crouched down and held it sideways where the water flow was fastest. It filled immediately. Cally watched as he replaced the cap and held the bottle up to the light. The liquid was opaque, a pale grey. He tilted it backwards and forwards and a rainbow-colored film glistened at the surface. He handed her the bottle.

"I wouldn't fancy drinking that," she said, "That screams poison."

"Here, hold it while I take a photo." Giles got out his phone.

"Don't throw it back," Cally said after he'd taken the picture. "Let's keep it."

"Good idea."

Cally focused on the stream as Giles re-stowed the

water bottle in the backpack.

"Someone must have built this pipe. I mean, they must have blasted out the rock to put it through," she said.

"Right. Or maybe there was a natural tunnel they put the pipe into. Anyhow, that means someone's intentionally draining this dump. But where to?"

"The lake," Cally said. "It has to be going into the lake. That misty lake's definitely down the hill from here." She remembered how out of breath she'd been the previous day by the time they made it up to the waste-dump. "I'll bet you the pipe drains into the lake."

"You're sure the lake's over the other side?" Giles looked up the side of the quarry face and then back at Cally.

"Yes. Remember? The deer path went uphill before we got to this. We were trying to get a signal on your phone."

"Yep. Let's check. Time for more rock-climbing?" he said.

The climb out of the quarry was no stroll, but Cally felt her legs were getting used to this kind of activity. She made it to the top ahead of Giles and was first to find the path, the very deer-path that they had trodden the day before. She almost had her breath back when Giles caught up, breathing hard.

The sound of the ocean in the distance reassured her that they were going in the right direction as the path headed down between oaks and weeds. The sky above was clear, a bright blue like a kid's painting, with not a cloud in sight, but the smell was still pretty bad. Cally felt a throbbing above one eye, the beginnings of a head-ache, but she was too excited to take much notice. She was expecting to see the lake at any moment. After all, it had only been a few minutes-walk yesterday between the crater where they'd heard the ducks splash into the water and the waste dump. She ran to the next ridge and stopped dead.

Cally did a double take. The scene that met her eyes was not what she'd expected. She looked up at the cloud-less sky, and then down, down into thick, grey fog. It was like looking into a witch's cauldron. It was as if a spell had been cast and they'd been transported back in time to the previous day.

"That's so weird," she said.

"What? The fog?" Giles seemed unperturbed as he caught up with her. "Yeah, that happens around the lakes near us in Albany too. The mist takes forever to clear in the mornings. Come on, we've got to find a way down. We don't even know for sure there's water down there."

"I know there is," said Cally. "Remember the birds

yesterday?" She started forward. She wanted to get down first.

As she scrambled, Cally felt dampness creeping over her. It was as if they'd walked into the refrigerated section of the grocery store on a boiling hot day. The shale-covered rock was moistened by the mist, and the fog got thicker as she climbed down. The noxious smell that she remembered from the previous day got stronger and stronger. It made the back of her throat tickle.

She coughed. "The stink's even worse here," she said.

Giles cleared his throat as he clambered behind her but said nothing.

In a particularly steep stretch, Cally leaned back into the hillside. She put her weight on her right foot, but it slipped away from under her. She tried to dig her left foot into the slope, but that slid too. She landed on her butt and almost bit her tongue as her top and bottom teeth slammed together.

"Owww," she said and reached out to stop her fall. But the rock that she grabbed on to came away in her hand. She tried again—grabbed for the next, and then the next. She felt a rising panic. Gravel and dirt started flying along with her, a human landslide.

"Cally!" she heard Giles shout.

She slid faster and faster down the smooth rock face and felt the cold air rushing past as her forward momentum increased. She saw a dark C-shaped form, a tree root maybe? and lunged at it. The fingers of her right hand clamped around the root, and it took her weight. She cried out as the full force of her motion ripped at her shoulder. She held on with all her remaining strength as her body swung outwards, then sideways and back. Her chin slammed into the rock. The world went black.

Chapter

8

"Cally, Cally!"

She heard the voice above the ringing in her ears. Giles' face was fading in and out in her vision, his breath warm in her face. She opened her eyes and tried to sit up.

"No. Stay down." His arm was gentle on her chest. "Stay still."

Cally sank back. The ringing began to recede. She looked up. Above was the dark shadow of the cliff and fog. She was lying in mud.

"What happened?"

"You rolled all the way down after you banged into that rock."

"Yeah, I remember the rock." Her jaw hurt. She tried opening and closing her mouth. The pain radiated from her chin.

"Where does it hurt?" He crouched over her. She felt

like the old lady they had found the day before. But no, that wasn't right. That old lady had not been conscious. Cally felt only too conscious, particularly in the chin region. She sat up.

"I'm OK," she told him. She shrugged her shoulders. The right one felt sore. She remembered swinging on the tree root. "I feel like I've just done an obstacle course, with ropes."

Giles sat back on his heels. He was staring at her. She focused on his face. It was ghostly pale, eyes wide, pupils gazing back into hers. She'd never seen him before, she thought. Not really SEEN him. He was unguarded, concerned. And he was concerned about HER. She felt better at the thought. "Really, I'm OK," she said, and she struggled to her feet.

"Wow." She took in the view. "So, there's the water."

The cliff face was separated from the water's edge by only a few feet of shale and sand. There was no vegetation to be seen, not that they could see very far. The fog hung over the scene like a curtain. "There's no way to know how big it is," she said. "I mean, is it a lake or a pond?"

"No idea," Giles agreed. "But whatever it is, it's not clean. Look at the slime on those rocks." He put his hand into the water and pulled it out. He rubbed his fingers together. "It's oily."

"Yuck," said Cally. "And look, over there!" She pointed

to the water's edge where it lapped against a natural curved inlet formed from rocks. Bobbing there on the surface was a collection of spindle shaped forms - elegant long white tail-fins, shimmering ivory scales, dorsal fins lying flat against the water surface. A shoal of dead fish.

"Oh my god." Giles pulled his backpack off his shoulder and pulled out his phone.

"I don't think I fancy a swim in there," she said.

While Giles took photos and collected another water sample in the other bottle, Cally had a chance to brush herself off and stretch out her bruised body.

"You OK? Ready to head back?" he asked. "Or should we walk around a bit first to see how big the lake is? The mist should lift soon."

Cally's head was throbbing, her face ached and the smell emanating from the lake was making breathing a struggle. She put her hand over her nose.

"Can't you map-quest that?" she said.

"I can't get a decent signal here, remember?"

"OK." Best just to be honest, she thought. "I vote we go. I can't stand the stink."

Giles picked up the backpack. "Good call," he said and started back up the slope.

The mist was thinning as they made their way up. Cally wondered how she was going to explain the bruise on her chin to her mom. She was trying to imagine the conversation when Giles stopped climbing.

"Shh," he hissed.

She stopped moving and listened. Distant but unmistakable. The rumble of deep voices. Above them, getting closer.

Giles moved down next to her, his finger to his lips. The rocks above formed a natural overhang. They pushed themselves into the hillside, backs to the cliff face, and waited. Cally could no longer hear voices, but heavy foot-falls crunched on stones. Then silence. She listened. Was that heavy breathing? Right above them? The sound of monsters who haunted the lake? Don't be stupid, she thought. More like out-of-condition adults doing exercise.

Giles said nothing, but his eyes met hers and held her gaze. His stare communicated DO NOT MOVE.

She suppressed a shiver. Thoughts of ghosts, ghouls, demons. Then…

"Pretty thick today."

"No worse than last week."

Deep voices. Two men. Nothing paranormal about them. Cally held her breath. The second voice spoke again.

"Let's get on with the depth measurements and get out."

"Hold on, I need to…" His words were lost in a paroxysm of coughing, followed by the sound of hacking spit.

"You should quit."

"Stuff that. It's not the smokes. It's the fumes."

"Put your mask on then."

"Fine."

"OK? Let's go."

As the voices receded into the distance Giles and Cally scrambled back up to the path. Cally caught sight of the back of two forms. But it wasn't their disparate heights that Cally noticed. It was the fact that they were both dressed from head to toe in white coveralls, complete with hoods. One was carrying a long stick.

"That's what I saw yesterday!" she whispered to Giles. "It wasn't deer, it was those guys."

"Shhh," Giles said. "Let's get out of here. Thank god they went that way. Come on!"

He headed off back the way they had come, the green backpack bouncing on his back. Cally glanced once more in the direction the men had taken and then raced after him.

They hurried on, making as little noise as possible, until they came to the flattened area of brush that lead between the trees back to the stone wall. The orange jacket was still visible on the top of the barbed wire.

"Those guys must have come in somewhere else," she said. "They had no idea we were there."

"Right, let's keep it that way," said Giles. He climbed up over the wire and held onto the No Trespassing sign while he reached out a hand for Cally. Together they jumped down on the other side. Cally felt a jolt of pain spread from her jaw right to the back of her skull as she landed. She breathed in hard. No need to draw attention to it, she thought.

"Here, stick this in your basket." Giles hadn't noticed anyway. He handed her the backpack and dragged his windbreaker off the fence. Cally retrieved her bike from behind the bushes. Glad we hid them, she thought, as she crammed the backpack into the basket. Giles was not far behind. In seconds they were heading down the hill.

Chapter

9

They were almost at the old lady's driveway when Cally slammed on her brakes.

"Hold up," she shouted to Giles. He looked back over his shoulder and came to a screeching halt.

"What the hell…" he shouted.

"I just had a thought," she said. "I want to check something out."

"What?" His *what* sounded more like *this better be good* to Cally's ears. But it WAS a good idea. Giles dismounted his bike and pushed it back up to join her.

"You remember that smell in the kitchen the old lady's house? When we were waiting for the ambulance?"

Giles nodded.

"Well, I think it was the same as the smell by the lake. And those men were talking about fumes, and about wearing masks. That smell has got to be toxic."

"Right." Giles took an exaggerated sniff. "But there's no smell here."

"Yeah, but let's just go and check around the house."

"If there's no one there, you mean? We can't just march inside."

"No, but we can go on the front porch. It smelled bad there too yesterday. Come on. It won't take long."

Cally started to push her bike up the drive. "Come on. It's your project," she shouted behind her.

"OK, Miss Smarty-Pants," he said, starting to follow.

They pushed their bikes along the curve in the drive. The pine trees cast long shadows. "That's not a bad smell," said Giles. He nodded at the trees.

Cally stood still. She lifted a finger to her lips, "Shh," and then pointed ahead.

A car, a yellow VW beetle, was parked in the drive. Cally was about to turn her bike around when the front door of the house opened and a woman sprang out.

"Hi," she said. "Are you lost?" A loud voice. She walked towards them opening a can of soda.

Cally stared, even though she knew it was rude to stare. This was no ordinary lady. Her hair was long, straight and the same garish yellow as the VW Beetle, but her bangs were bright purple, contrasting with her gloss-red lips. She had a beautiful face. How could anyone so made-up look so natural? She could definitely be a pop star, Cally thought.

"No," Cally told her. "We were here yesterday. The

dog led us here. We found someone collapsed and called the police."

"Oh wow! It was you two? You're my heroes! That was my mom you rescued."

She ran towards them and enveloped Cally in a powerfully scented hug. Ginger ale splashed, Cally's bike fell sideways, and Giles grabbed its handlebars.

"Oh, sorry," she said. "That was clumsy of me."

"How is your mom doing?" Cally asked, as she extricated herself and wiped soda off her shoulder.

"She's OK. No broken bones, thank god, but a wicked headache. They're not sure what caused her to fall. They're keeping her in for observation for a day or two." The words tumbled out. Cally had never heard anyone speak so rapidly. The lady hardly paused for breath. "Here, prop your bikes over there and come in. I was just going to sit out on Moms' porch when you showed up. She's got like ginger ale and diet coke in her fridge. And maybe tea. I hoped for cider but I couldn't find any. Which would you like?"

"Ginger ale, thanks," said Cally. Giles nodded. He appeared to have been rendered speechless by the occasion.

"You two sit down over there." She pointed to the two wooden rockers on the porch. "I'll be right back." And she was gone back inside the house.

"Wow," said Giles. Cally wasn't sure whether his response was to the lady's whirlwind conversation, or to her amazing good looks. They sat down in their appointed places but had no time for discussion before she returned.

"Introductions!" she declared as she handed over the drinks. "I'm Petra, short for Petronella Stewart. And my mom's Polly Stewart. I call her Moms, not Mom, cos she's my adoptive mom not my actual mom. So, you must be Pascale and Giles."

"It's Cally," Cally interrupted.

"Right, Cally and Giles. Jimmy Whistler, Officer Whistler, his son Greg was in my grade at school, told me your names," she said by way of explanation. She paused long enough to engage them with the widest smile, bright white teeth and even brighter eyes, first directed straight at Cally, and then, with equal intensity, at Giles. "It's just amazing, what you did. Amazing."

"Not really," said Cally. "It was her dog that saved her. He made us follow him."

"She's right," said Giles, finally woken from his stupor. "He almost tore my pants leg off. What's his name?"

"Solomon, Sol. He's a great dog," Petra agreed. "And yeah, he's clever, but he couldn't have called the ambulance. You two did that. And seriously, I don't know what would have happened if you hadn't found her." Petronella's face was suddenly serious. "See, I don't live here, I live in town, but I come to see her most days, because she's on her own. And she's too old to be on her own. Pops, that's what I called him, died a long time ago. But I was down in Portland all yesterday morning, so I hadn't checked in. And I feel really bad about that." She gave an involuntary shiver and brought the palm of her free hand over her heart. "I can't thank you enough."

Were those tears in her eyes? Cally wondered.

"Honestly, we didn't do that much." Giles shifted in his seat. "I was glad I had my phone with me."

Petra seemed to gather herself. She sat on the wide railing that ran around the deck. "So, you're here on vacation? Did you just happen to be walking up the cliff road when Sol found you?"

"Down it. We were walking back into town," Giles said.

Cally thought about their trek yesterday, and today's discoveries flashed into her mind. She pictured the leaking oil drums, the lake, the dead fish, the smell, the reason they'd made the detour to the cottage. She looked at Petra. "Can I ask you something?"

"Sure."

"Have you noticed a bad smell in the house? We both did yesterday."

Petra's eyes opened wide. "You smelled it too?" She jumped off the railing. "I was just walking round trying to get a fix on it, when you showed up. I thought it was just because the house had been closed up and Moms sometimes leaves stuff out for composting."

"Right. Yesterday it was worst in the kitchen, where we found your mom."

"Yes, I think so too. Come on in, let's see."

They followed Petra into the shade and cool of the kitchen. She'd opened the back door out to the yard.

"Here, let's close that."

Cally made her way to the sink under the kitchen window. It sparkled clean in the early afternoon sun that streamed in through the window. "This is where we smelled it worst yesterday," she said. She sniffed hard. "Maybe not so bad now." Then a thought struck her. She turned on the faucet and let it run. She stood back and breathed in.

"Christ. That's foul." Petra said behind her. She'd put her hand up to close off her nose.

"It's almost as bad as the lake smell," said Giles.

"It's the SAME as the lake," said Cally, unable to suppress a note of triumph in her voice. "Isn't it?" She looked at Giles for confirmation.

"Hang on, we can check," said Giles. He left the kitchen.

"What on earth are you two talking about?" asked Petra, turning off the faucet.

"It's a long story," said Cally. "But Giles and I were just up at the lake over the top of the hill, before we came here. The one near the Danger sign? Between there and the cliff. There's a big waste dump there too. And the whole area has this terrible stench."

"You mean Foggy Bottom?"

"Is that what you call it? About half a mile away, up the hill?"

Giles returned with the green backpack. He set it down on the kitchen table and extracted one of the water-bottles. "Water from the lake," he said at Petra's questioning gaze.

"How do you know it's not the quarry one?" Cally asked.

"The quarry one was even dirtier looking. You could see oil on the top, remember?"

"Right."

He opened the screw top and took a long breath in. He breathed out, coughed and handed the bottle over to Cally. "You're right," he said.

Cally shook the bottle and took a sniff. "Gross," she said.

"Let me," said Petra. She turned on the faucet again, took a sniff. Closed it. Breathed out. Brought the bottle to her nose and inhaled again. "Christ almighty," she said. "That's bad. Let's go back outside."

Back in the fresh air they settled back into their seats with Petra perched on a foot stool in front of one of the rockers.

"So, is this really water from Foggy Bottom?" Petra began. She put the cap on the bottle and held it up to the light. "I used to swim in there when I was a kid."

"We didn't know it was called that," said Giles. "But it's a good name. We've been there twice and it was foggy both times."

"Yes, it always used to be. It was a fun place to hang out. There were four of us from school spent pretty much the whole summer there when I was like, eight, when I was still living with my real mom. We'd catch frogs and fish and mess around. We managed to convince ourselves it was haunted. So, Hide and Go Seek was pretty scary. And then there was Foggy Bottom Monster. Charlie Parker said it grabbed his leg while he was swimming. We all ran away. It was all part of the scariness, really fun." Petra smiled.

"So, did you have to climb over walls and barbed wire to get there then?" Giles asked.

"No, definitely not. There was nothing to stop us walking in, as far as I remember, not that a wall or two would have stopped us. I was pretty wild." She grinned.

"That *No Trespassing* sign is pretty recent, I think."

"And was the water clean then?" asked Cally.

"Sure, as far as I remember. Like I said, we swam in it when it was hot, and it definitely didn't smell like that." She handed the bottle back to Giles.

"Was there a quarry with waste dumped in it there then, right next to the lake?"

"Quarry yes. No waste dump. I remember there was a really pretty stream going through."

"OK. So, that's definitely the same place," said Cally. "Look, if the water from the faucet smells like that, could your mom have been poisoned by it?" This thought had been germinating in her mind since she'd started down the hill. After all, her neighbor back in Vermont had had their water well poisoned with fertilizer from the local farms. "Does your mom have a well?"

"Sure. She's too far out of Penzance for mains water. There's not enough well water to keep the vegetable garden watered. It was baths once a week when I was at high school." Petra smiled and then became serious. "But you're right. I'd never thought of that. And she's said to me before that there was a bad smell sometimes. I never really bothered about it. I just thought she hadn't been taking the trash out often enough or the composting was the problem."

"So, your mom never complained about the water?" Cally asked.

"No. But if it got bad gradually maybe she wouldn't have noticed. And I always have soda or beer here. I never drink her tea or coffee when I'm over. I'm not into hot drinks. But a poisoned water supply, that's what could have made her ill." She breathed heavily. "Wow, that really could be it." She collapsed back, her stillness in stark contrast to her previous non-stop activity.

Giles glanced down at his phone and back up at Cally. "We'd better get going."

"Can I keep the samples?" Petra was wound up again. "I should maybe send some to the state lab, to get it tested. I've got a friend there who'll help."

"Sure," they said in unison.

"The one we haven't opened yet, is from the quarry," Giles added. "That smells just as bad."

"Maybe you shouldn't open it until you get it tested, in case the smell gets out," Cally said.

"Good thinking," Petra nodded. "And I'm going to go up to Foggy Bottom tomorrow to take a look for myself. My boyfriend works for the Penzance Press. I'll bet he'll be interested. Do you want to come too?" She was back on her feet, leading the way back to the bikes.

Giles looked at Cally.

She shook her head. "There's one problem. While we were climbing up from the lake we saw these two guys. They were doing something down there. Maybe inspectors? They had these white coveralls on."

"Did they see you?"

"No. We hid." Giles said. "See, we knew we were trespassing…" he added by way of explanation.

Petra seemed unperturbed. "OK. So tomorrow we won't trespass. I'll ask Shamus to bring his drone."

"Drone?" Giles said eagerly.

"Yes. Well, not his, exactly. It belongs to the paper. The reporters use it to get pictures for their articles without having to trespass. And we *borrow* it sometimes to get great overhead pics at gigs. Don't tell his boss though." She smiled a kid-like smile. "So, do you want to come along?"

Giles and Cally exchanged glances. "Sure," she said.

"Great. We'll pick you up at say 10 o'clock. You're at the Penzance Hotel?"

Cally nodded. She retrieved her bike. "Umm, there's one other thing." She glanced at Giles.

"Yes?" Petra asked.

"Our parents…" Cally began, then paused.

"They don't actually know about this, about everything, that we were trespassing…" Giles finished.

"No problem. We don't need to mention that. My lips are sealed." She mimed locking her lips and throwing away the key. "But I am looking forward to meeting them."

"We could just say you wanted to show us around Penzance?" suggested Giles.

"Great. Great idea. OK. That'll work. See you in the lobby at 10 tomorrow. Thanks again for rescuing Moms."

"No problem," said Cally.

As they cycled back down the drive, Giles caught up with Cally and stood up on his pedals.

"Wow," he said. "Cool, huh Pascale?"

Chapter

10

As Cally entered their shared bedroom that evening after supper, her mom jumped off the bed and held out her red cell phone.

"It's your dad."

"Hi, Dad." His face smiled at her from the screen. He was outside, bathed in sunlight, maybe on a balcony, his baseball cap on, his face framed by green fronds and tropical looking plants against a backdrop of blue sky. He was leaning back in a chair with his hands behind his head, and his white t-shirt looked startlingly bright. Must be Facetiming from his laptop, she thought.

"Hi sweetie. What happened to your chin?"

Cally turned her head so that her face was no longer lit by the bedside light. He wouldn't have noticed at all, she thought, except that her mom had insisted in cleaning the wound and dressing it with a band-aid.

"I smashed into a rock," she'd said, just the whitest of lies. Her mom had accepted that and assumed she'd been clambering *over* rocks rather than down a rock face.

"Did you already go for your run?" she asked, anxious to get away from the subject of the fall. Her dad looked overheated. The part of his face that wasn't covered by his short stubby black beard or his baseball cap was glistening with sweat. Some of her earliest memories were of running with her dad. Her mom had never wanted to go running with them, even when they only went about half a mile and stopped for ice cream on the way back.

"I sure did. Have to get it in early here. It's too hot and humid later on."

"What time is it?"

"Just after seven in the morning. So, how's the vacation going?"

"Great. Did Mom tell you that Giles and I had to call the police to help an old lady who'd collapsed?"

"She did. I swelled up with pride." He touched his chest for emphasis. "It sounds like you did the right thing. Good for you. Is she OK?"

"I think so. We met her daughter and she said she was being kept in hospital for observation." Cally smiled. She'd just had a flash of inspiration. "But we wouldn't have been able to help or do anything without Giles' phone," she said.

"Right, I guess so." Her dad's voice slowed. Cally hurried on.

"So don't you think I should have one? What if I'd been on my own?"

Got you! she thought. She glanced up to see whether her mom had heard this. She was stretched out on her bed, eyes closed. Maybe asleep?

"Hmm."

She watched as her dad did his characteristic beard-rubbing move. "Well, I'll give that idea some thought," he said.

This was definite progress. Giving things *thought* generally had good outcomes, Cally knew. No point pushing it though.

"Anyway, more important right now is the Singapore thing." He clearly wanted to get back onto safe ground.

"Mom only told me about it yesterday," she said.

"I know, I'm sorry. We didn't want to worry you until it was certain."

"But why wouldn't I go with you?" The whole thing was pretty astonishing, she thought.

"I know. Maybe it's a crazy idea. But your mom feels so sad for you. She knows you hated school last year."

He didn't know the half of it, Cally thought. She grimaced as she remembered the feeling of trying to hide in the back row during music, terrified the music teacher Mrs Snow would pick on her to sing.

Her dad was now pouring himself a glass of orange juice. "She just wants you to have choices," he said.

"Right. Singapore sounds cool. And Giles' school is really good for math."

"Well, I'm glad you're looking at the positives." He glanced down at his glass, then back at her. "I went to see the school here. It's a great campus."

"I saw some pictures online, with Giles."

"Well I saw it in person, yesterday. You'd be in 7th grade and move into 8th after summer."

"What are the kids like?" she said.

"Honestly Cally, it's hard for me to tell. Different from Vermont, that's for sure."

"Why?"

"Well for one thing, they're not all white. Maybe half the kids are Asian. They seemed happy and chatty. I looked in on one class, and they were learning Chinese."

"Chinese?"

"Right."

"What's the point of me learning Chinese? For just one year?"

"It's a great idea to learn Chinese. Anyway, that's beside the point," her dad hurried on. He clearly didn't want to get into an argument. "I thought the kids looked like they were having fun. They seemed to be practicing for some sort of play."

What else should she ask? Cally wondered. "What's the cafeteria like?"

"A bit like yours at Cloverdale, but sunnier. Same sort of choices of food, maybe more rice and Asian stuff. And you can go outside to eat."

"Do they have a chess club? And athletics?"

"No chess club, I asked about that, but you and I, we could do that together. Remember we used to?"

He sounded a bit sad, she thought.

"And running, yes. Not so much long-distance stuff. It's too hot. But they have a track, and most of the kids do some sport. They've got a great pool, so you could get into swimming."

Cally tried to imagine herself there. "Where would we live?" she asked.

"That's one really good thing. There's faculty housing just a few streets away. We'll have this great home, loads of rooms and a shared pool. And there'd be no need for you to catch the school bus."

"That's good."

"OK, so chat to Giles about Albany. Remember you'll be here in Singapore for all the summer vacation, what-ever you decide. Right?"

"Right."

"We'll take a trip to Malaysia then. See real jungle."

"Awesome." An unexpected thrill ran through her.

"So, try to think about what you're interested in. If its math and science, Albany might be best; if its languages and geography and world stuff, then a year at school here could be great."

"But what about weekends? I mean if I stay here?" Her dad never seemed to think of the practical things.

"You know you love Aunt Beth, and she loves you. She's keen to take you under her wing again. And I think she reckons Giles might like the company. What do you think about him?"

"He's not the chattiest. But he's cool." She thought of his striking eyes, how his grin lit up his face. The pink heat was rising up her face again. "I still don't know him, really."

"Right. So look, sweetie. It's a big choice. But you're up to it. And it's only for a year."

A year felt like an age to her. "And then I go back to Cloverdale?"

"That's the plan."

"Wow. Seriously Dad, Wow. But, if I stay here, I wouldn't see you and Mom 'till summer."

"Look Cally-bear. If you stay in the US, Mom and I would come to visit every month. One or other of us. I'll have to come back sometimes to keep my grad students on track anyway."

"And I'd have my own phone, so I can Facetime with you." She smiled at her dad. Her mom was off the bed and heading across the room.

"Very clever." Her father made a mock grimace and sighed. "I give in. Yes, you'll have your own phone, whatever you decide."

Cally's mom held her hand out for the phone.

"Great!" A win! "OK. Mom's grabbing the phone. Bye Dad. See you next week."

"Love you, Cally. Have a good time in Maine. Email or Facetime if you want to chat."

"Will do." My own phone at last, she thought. Yes!

Chapter

11

Next morning, Cally had just finished breakfast when she saw a green pick-up truck pull up outside. Petra hopped out, followed by a guy. Has to be Shamus, Cally thought. He was, surprisingly, a very conventional-looking man, clean-shaven, blue-eyed, Scandinavian features. He presented a stark contrast to Petra, who led the way towards the foyer, dressed in a white t-shirt and blue jeans with red suspenders that matched her lipstick in color and clashed strikingly with her purple bangs.

"Mom, Aunt Beth," Cally said, as she got up from the table, "Petra and Shamus are here." She pointed out of the restaurant window. "D'you want to come and say hello before we go?"

Cally had already filled her mom and Aunt Beth in on their plans for the morning. In exchange for their parents' permission to go on a guided tour of Penzance with Petra and Shamus during the morning, she and Giles had

promised that they would hang out with the moms in
the afternoon. Cally didn't mind at all, since she felt a bit
guilty about telling only partial truths and about spending so little time with the parents so far this vacation.
But, on the other hand, her mom had said she wanted her
to get to know Giles.

"Sure," said her mom and Beth in unison. Giles was
on his feet waving through the window.

They met in the lobby. Petra was already talking as
she bounded across and reached out a hand to shake.

"You must be Cally's mom. You look so much like
Cally," she began.

Cally wondered how Petra could possibly have
guessed which of the sisters was her mom. Maybe it was
that she and her mom both kept their hair tied back,
while Aunt Beth's always flowed loose. Aunt Beth always
looked much more romantic. Her mom's nod was all that
Petra needed to continue.

"You must be so proud of them both. I don't think they
realize, but I have to tell you, that they probably saved my
Moms' life."

Cally's mom opened her mouth to speak. "How is she
do...?"

"She's got to stay in hospital for tests," said Petra. "But
she seems much better. No more falls or faints or whatever it was. She's not a frail woman, and she's not one to

stay in bed, but she still looks so pale. You should under-
stand Moms doesn't take help easily, and she never lets
me stay over at her place and so that's why I wasn't there.
She says it's too much of an imposition. I live over there
on Market Street by the harbor. But still I feel bad because I should have been there. And I wasn't. So, honestly
Mrs. Mountbatten…"

"Janie," her mom interjected. "And this is Beth, Giles'
step-mom."

Petra smiled and nodded at Beth as she talked.

"So, I owe a huge debt of gratitude to Giles and Cally.
SO…" she paused long enough for an intake of breath
and for Shamus to raise his eyebrows, "We," she moved
to one side and indicated her boyfriend, "me and Shamus
that is, would love to take them around town and maybe
to our favorite place for a morning ice cream, by way of
thanks."

Shamus' grin was contagious. He was clearly used to
the effect Petra had on people and found it a huge joke.
Her mom and Beth just smiled back at them in a daze.
Petra kept on talking as he ushered them into the truck.
She sure knows how to deal with parents, Cally thought.

"So just so you know, you've got the best kids on the
planet. We'll have them back by lunchtime."

"Sounds good," said Cally's mom. "So glad they could
help."

"See you back here, then," her mom said as Cally and Giles climbed up onto the narrow bench that was the back seat of the truck.

They headed out of town and up the cliff road. The seat bounced up and down, as if unattached to the truck's base. Cally held onto the back of the driver's seat. She hoped she wasn't going to get carsick. Giles' attention was focused on the drone that Petra had pressed into his lap before she'd climbed into the front seat. It was slate grey, shaped like a robotic tarantula, except that it had four legs instead of eight and a camera for a body. He held it delicately, like he was holding a precious, thousand-piece Lego construction.

"This is so cool," he said as he turned it around in his hands. "How does it take pictures?"

"I control it from the remote-control unit," Shamus said. He nodded toward what looked like a black Nintendo controller where it lay in the space between the front seats. "My phone is connected to that, so I can see on the screen what the drone is seeing. It's basically a flying camera."

"It takes a bit of skill though," said Petra. She raised her head from her cell-phone. "Remember, Shame?"

"Don't remind me."

"What happened?" asked Giles.

"Last year we were at a bluegrass concert down in

Portland, and Shamus was taking photos for the paper's write-up. I told you, he works for the Penzance Post. So, he was stung by a wasp right on the eyebrow. It got caught behind his sunglasses and I had to take over the controls. He literally threw that thing at me," she pointed at the controller, "along with his glasses. It was chaos. Utter chaos." They both laughed.

"So, I'm not a gamer," she continued. "Never have been. I had no clue what any of those controls do. Long story short, a guy got a nasty surprise when the drone landed on his head."

"No damage done," said Shamus. "At least not to the drone."

"But we did have to buy the guy and his buddy a couple of drinks," Petra agreed.

"I hope we can get some better pictures than the ones I took," said Giles.

"Why do you need pictures?" asked Petra.

Cally realized they'd never explained to Petra why they'd been up at Foggy Bottom the previous day. She let Giles fill Shamus and Petra in on his school assignment, before asking him her own question.

"The photos weren't any good?"

"Not great. Some of the close-ups from the dump are OK, but there wasn't enough light down by the lake. And the phone's no good for landscapes."

"That's where the drone comes in," said Shamus. "I'm real interested to see this place. Sounds like it could be a great story. I must have driven past that sign a hundred times and never thought to go look."

"And if it's got something to do with Moms' illness," Petra said, "It's going to be big news in Penzance."

"What did you do with the water samples?" asked Cally.

"Nothing yet," she said. "But when we get back I'll send them off to Lillian at the Department of Environment Protection lab in Augusta. And I'll send her some of Moms' water too. We do need some more evidence."

"I need some fresh air," said Cally. She pressed the button to roll her car window down as the familiar dizziness that preceded carsickness took hold. She wished she hadn't eaten breakfast.

"No problem," Shamus said.

"We're nearly there," said Giles. He pointed ahead. "Look, you can see the skull and crossbones sign. This is where we climbed over the wall."

Shamus slowed down. "OK. There's not enough room to park here."

"There used to be a pull-off a bit further up," said Petra. "I don't remember all this barbed wire and stuff being here when we were kids."

Shamus put his foot down. The truck lurched forwards.

"It's just round this bend," Petra said.

Sure enough, a little further along the stone and barbed wire wall diverged from the road. The space in front was filled with tire tracks that had gouged deep ridges in the dirt. The tracks lead to a wide wire-mesh gate held closed by a rusty padlock. A roll of thin barbed wire ran along the top and continued down to the fence on both sides.

"I guess they don't want visitors," said Shamus. He pulled the truck off the road onto the grass verge just beyond the entrance.

"Nothing to stop us parking here though," said Petra. "So, let's give Derek an airing."

"Derek?" asked Cally.

"Derek the Drone," said Shamus as he climbed out.

Cally and Giles watched with admiration as Shamus put the drone through its paces. In the space of ten minutes it mapped out the area with low magnification panoramic shots of the oil-drum crater near to the gate where they stood. They crowded around Shamus' phone to see the pictures.

"Wow. That crap wasn't there when we were kids," said

Petra. "It was like a fairy-tale place back then. Flowers and birds. And look at that pool, it's grim." She pointed to the spot where Cally had stood the day before. The camera had captured the black sheen on the surface of the marshy ground in a dramatic fashion.

"OK," said Shamus. "I think we've got enough from here. Now where do we go to see Foggy Bottom?"

"It's over that way," said Petra and Cally together. Shamus directed the drone down and away from the quarry. Petra manned the phone.

"No joy," she said as she showed the screen to Giles and Cally. "Too misty."

"Just like yesterday," said Cally.

Shamus went back to the controls and brought the drone back overhead.

"We could go down the same way we did yesterday," Giles said as Shamus brought Derek in to land. He was clearly not ready to give up. "At least we can get better close-ups."

"Right, and I want to see how the lake looks now too," said Petra. "Especially after everything you've told us. Then straight off to the ice cream parlor."

They left the van parked, and Giles led the way back down the road on foot to where they had scaled the fence the previous day. Ten minutes later they were all at the top of the slope where Cally had slid down to the lake. Even at the top, the smell was strong, throat-catching.

Petra sniffed and pulled a face. "You're right, it's really bad," she said. "But look." She pointed over toward the ocean. "The fog's clearing."

Sure enough, a fresh breeze had started to blow, dissolving the mist ahead of it. In the space of a minute, an expanse of water the size of several soccer fields was revealed, lined on all sides by steep, tree and bracken- covered hills.

"Oh my god," said Petra.

"What?" asked Cally. "Can you see the dead fish?" She looked down towards the edge of the lake.

"No, it's not that," said Petra. It's the lake itself. Its huge. I swear that Foggy Bottom was not this big when I was a kid."

"That's funny," said Shamus. "Usually things look smaller than your childhood memories of them, like our kindergarten playground."

"Right, I know that." Petra turned to Giles and Cally. "We went to the same kindergarten," she said, by way of explanation. "And he's right, the playground looks tiny now." She turned back to survey the scene. "But honestly there used to be a sandy and stony beach pretty much all the way round the lake. But not now. Look, over there, the trees go right down to the water's edge." She pointed across the other side. "See there, they're in the water."

Cally followed her gaze. The lake did indeed look like a reservoir. The only beach area she could see was down below them, where she and Giles had explored the previous day.

"I wonder if there's any old photos in the Penzance library of how Foggy Bottom used to look." Shamus said. "I'll look into that. But right now, let's put the drone through its paces."

"Look, down there," said Giles. "Get photos of those." The dead fish had not moved. They formed a shimmering V-shaped phalanx bobbing in the water next to a rocky outcrop.

"Those are the fish we saw yesterday," Cally said. "And I found a dead bird the first day we were here, over by the cliff." Cally had a flashback to the moment she'd sunk her hand into the seagull's flesh and feathers. She shivered.

"This is some serious shit," said Shamus.

"It's poisonous, for sure," said Petra. "And I know it didn't used to be like this. It's just so sad."

"Ready for that ice cream?" asked Petra as they walked back up the road towards the pick-up truck. It was a pretty obvious attempt to lighten the mood, and Cally felt grateful for it.

"Always ready for ice cream," she said.

"Especially if they've got Rocky Road," agreed Giles.

"The place I have in mind has the best ice cream in Maine. And more important, it doesn't just cater to tourists. Mollie's stays open in September."

"OK," said Cally, picking up her pace up the hill. She saw the corner ahead. "Almost there."

She stopped dead in her tracks.

"Careful," said Giles as he cradled the drone against his chest. "I could have dropped it."

"Here, I'll take it," said Shamus.

"Shh," Cally said. "Look!" She pointed ahead. The truck was as they had left it, but it was dwarfed by a black tanker trailer that was in the process of reversing through the opened gate. Cally could just make out the driver of the truck. His head was turned towards his wing mirror, too concentrated on the job in hand to notice them. A second figure's overall-clad legs were visible moving around on the other side of the tanker. "Right hand down, Saul," he shouted as they watched. "Straighten up." And then, "OK. Go, go, go." The truck's engine revved and then... beep, beep, beep, the sound of the tanker reversing.

"Quick," said Petra. She pulled Cally and Giles back behind the hedge so they could not be seen. Shamus moved forward and peered around the corner.

"What's happening?"

"They're uncoiling a hose," he said. "Like a fire-truck's

hose. It's attached to the bottom of the tanker."

"Where are they going with it?"

"Looks like they're heading for the quarry."

"They haven't turned the engine off. I'll bet they're going to pump whatever's in the tanker into the quarry," said Cally.

"You stay here," said Shamus, turning to Giles and Cally. "I'll pick you up once we've got the truck."

"Wait for me. I'll come too," said Petra. She was up behind him before he could object. Giles and Cally waited out of sight.

The minutes passed like hours.

"What's taking so long?" Giles wondered out loud.

"I'm going to have a look," said Cally. She edged to the corner, crouched down and put her head around. "He's flying the drone!" she said.

The words had barely left her mouth when the tanker's engine cut out and a deep voice rumbled, "What the hell do you think you're doing?"

Shamus' voice was too low for Cally to hear his reply. But she watched him hand the remote control to Petra, and dig into his jeans pocket. He took out his wallet. "I think he's showing them his ID," she said. "And Petra's got the drone."

"Don't let them see you," said Giles. "Let them handle it." He pulled Cally back out of sight.

A minute later they heard the doors of the pick-up truck bang shut and its engine roar to life. The next moment it appeared around the corner.

"Quick, get in," said Petra, as it drew up alongside. "Don't bang the doors."

They climbed aboard and waited until they were further down the road before slamming the doors shut.

"Let's go and get that ice cream," said Petra. Shamus put his foot down and the truck accelerated down the hill.

"What happened back there?" asked Cally.

"You guessed right, Cally. They are dumping stuff into the stream. Shamus got some footage of them doing it, before they caught sight of us."

"Derek the Drone triumphs again!" Shamus smiled back at them, and the truck lurched sideways.

"Eyes on the road for christ's sake," said Petra. "We've got to get these two back in one piece." She patted him on the knee. "But it was pretty good investigative reporting, I have to say. You stood your ground really well."

"Who were they?" asked Giles.

"Good question. Did you see there wasn't any logo on the tanker? But the big guy's coverall had his name badge on it. They work for Tanglebell Oil and Gas," said Shamus.

"And boy was he pissed with Shame for flying the

drone. He tried to tell us we were trespassing." Petra put her feet up on the dashboard as she spoke.

Shamus nodded. "Even more pissed when I told him I worked for the Penzance Post. But I wasn't doing anything illegal. We weren't on their land, at least not when they saw us. This is going to make a great story."

"It's Tanglebell Oil and Gas that's doing something illegal. That water is killing fish and the air's foul and if they really are making Moms' well-water smell that bad, it has to be illegal and we have to be able to stop them." Petra banged her feet up and down to emphasize the point. She drew breath again and turned around in her seat. "You guys are the best, you know that? Not only did you rescue Moms, you might have solved the mystery of why she's ill."

"And they've given me a great lead for a story," said Shamus.

"All in all, a good reason to go get ice cream," added Petra. I'll bet you've never seen an ice cream parlor like this one." Petra bounced in her seat with the enthusiasm of a five-year old.

Chapter

12

It wasn't the ice cream that was so surprising, but the location. Cally could hardly believe it. Shamus had parked the truck at the top of a hill, on a non-descript side-street with nothing to recommend it except for a nail salon and a take-away Thai restaurant. The buildings had somehow been constructed on a steep incline. They'd climbed out of the truck and followed him down toward a wooden bridge. It was an unusual bridge in that it looked like an old-fashioned cart path, literally just planks of wood with no railing on either side.

"Are we going to cross the bridge?" she asked Shamus.

"No," he said, "the ice cream parlor's just around the corner at the bottom of the hill on this side. But first you've got to see this. It's Penzance's best kept secret."

As they approached the bridge, Cally noticed the background noise getting louder. At first it sounded like the flying drone, then more like a sit-on lawnmower, then louder and louder. Rushing water.

"Is that the Penzance River?" she shouted to Shamus.

"No, its Scarpside brook, a tributary of the Penzance. Look!"

They'd reached the bottom of the slope. The road turned sharp left and there they found themselves at the bottom of a fifty-foot waterfall. The sun glinted on the water at the top, making rainbow arcs. The torrents splashed over granite rocks and broken tree trunks that had lodged in the space, and then came vertically down, down towards them into the narrow steep-sided gully beneath the bridge. The noise of the water reverberated on the stone walls, drowning out any conversation. Cally felt a tug on her arm, and turned to follow the others.

"Pretty cool," she said, as they escaped from the noise into the ice cream parlor.

While Petra bought the ice creams, Cally, Shamus and Giles sat down at a circular table adorned with a red-and-white checkered table-cloth. They were the only customers in the shop.

"So, you and Petra have always lived here?" she asked Shamus. Giles was buried in his cell-phone.

"Right." He took off his jacket, green with a tartan lining, and hung it on the back of his chair. "Well, me all the time. Petra lived all around the state as a kid. But she's right, we were at kindergarten together."

"She said her mom's really her adopted mom?" asked Cally.

"Yeah, you should ask her about that."

"She doesn't mind talking about it?" Giles looked up from his screen.

So, he is listening to the conversation, thought Cally.

"Petra doesn't mind talking about anything," Shamus said with a grin. He looked up. "Looks like she needs a hand," he said.

Petra had two double scoop cones in one hand and was attempting to pick up two cups off the counter in the other. Shamus dashed over to help her.

After they had all settled down and Cally had had a couple of very satisfying licks at her pralines and cream ice cream, she wondered how to bring the topic up again. She was curious about Petra—about being a foster kid and having such a cool appearance. But before she could frame a question Petra had queries of her own.

"So how come you two are on vacation? Isn't school in session in Vermont?"

"Well, I'm in Vermont and Giles lives in Albany," Cally answered. "And you're right, school is in session. Our moms... well my mom, and Giles' step-mom," she corrected herself as she looked quickly at Giles. His head was down again. "They came up with this crazy scheme to get us to know each other better." Giles put his head up and she saw with some apprehension the black cloud back on his face. Better change the subject she thought and hurried on. "So, Shamus said that you moved around all over Maine when you were a kid?"

"Yeah. We lived here at first, me and my mom. We were in a trailer park on the coast road. I thought she was normal but it turned out she wasn't. She was a user."

Cally stopped eating her ice cream. She hadn't expected such frankness. She saw Giles' attention was also totally focused on Petra.

"Yeah," she continued with a sigh. "Drugs—a lot of them. They took me away when I was nine. Then it was four different foster families until I landed with Moms."

"God, that must have been terrible." Cally couldn't even begin to imagine it.

Petra shrugged and pushed her hair away from her face. "Terrible with her, terrible without her, honestly. So, anyway, now I work for a not-for-profit that goes around schools teaching kids about drug abuse and stuff. *Good Starts,* we're called. What I didn't get, I suppose. But then I did get lucky." Petra brightened. "More like *Good Endings* for me. Last three years at high school I was fostered with Moms back here in Penzance - Polly Stewart that is. She adopted me. Turns out she'd known my mom as a kid too. She really knew how to be a mom. Even to a teenager. That's why I should have been there when she collapsed."

"You're not to blame." Shamus took Petra's hand.

The sun came back into Petra's face, as quickly as it had left. Cally saw Giles' intent gaze. Was he thinking about his own mom?

"Didn't you want to get back to your own mom when you got out of foster care?" he asked.

"No chance," she said. Matter of fact. No hesitancy. "She overdosed. I was sixteen. It was bound to happen, sooner or later, I guess. So… I'm Petra Stewart now. Always will be. And being dragged away from my mom at nine taught me one thing - that you've got to hang on to those you love. So we've got to make sure Moms' water is safe."

Petra paused, an uncharacteristic silence. Shamus looked at his watch. "Eat up," he said. "Got to get you two back to your hotel. Time for me to get this story written up."

That afternoon was long and lazy. The sun shone brightly but a cool breeze sprang up as they walked down the road from the hotel. Since her mom and aunt were averse to climbing over the railing to the beach, Cally and Giles walked with them around the esplanade until they reached the stone steps down to the sand. They set up camp in a sun-trap near the harbor wall. The beach itself was deserted except for gulls that circled overhead and a flock of waders that darted their heads in and out of the water and stutter-stepped in the waves. All the action of the port seemed to happen on the other side of the pier, where they could see the masts and flags of fishing boats and pleasure craft and hear the sounds of engines revving, crates clanging and people shouting.

Cally felt no irritation at spending time lying on the beach with the parents, but Giles seemed to have retired again into his shell. While she chatted to her mom and Aunt Beth, he remained silent. He placed an empty soda can on a pile of sand twenty yards away and focused on hitting it with pebbles. Drawing back, just like a hermit crab, she thought.

"My turn," she shouted. Her first shot went way to the left of the target. But Giles refused to be drawn.

"I'm going for a wade," she said. Cally removed her shoes and socks and headed towards the water. She put an experimental toe in the foam.

"Yowl! It's freezing," she shouted. She turned and was surprised to find Giles right behind her. The sound of the water breaking on the shore must have drowned out his approach.

"It's not so bad," he said. "Come on."

Cally waded after him along the near-shore.

"Do you think those guys, the Tanglebell people, were really dangerous?" she asked as she drew alongside. Maybe she could cheer him up by talking about the morning.

Petra's parting words to them as they'd arrived back at the hotel at lunchtime had been, *I'll let you know how it goes. But no more trips to Foggy Bottom, you two.* Cally was glad that Petra and Shamus had taken everything so seriously, but she felt sad that their adventures were over. She wondered if that was what was dragging Giles down too.

"Nah, they were just doing their job," he said. "And it's private property. I guess they were under orders to scare people away."

"Probably. I can't believe Shamus told them about working for the Penzance Post," she said.

"How else was he going to explain the drone and, like he said, he wasn't trespassing when they saw us."

"Yes, I suppose… Yikee, the sea's freezing." Cally waded out of the water onto the wet sand.

"You need the warm seas of Singapore?" said Giles. He splashed after her.

Cally was glad to hear the fun was back in his voice. Maybe it was being around adults that bothered him, she thought, not the end of the Foggy Bottom adventure.

"So you think I should go?" she asked.

"Sure. I already told you. Way more fun than Albany. Fun," he repeated, "Aim for fun. That's what my mom told me."

"Your mom?" Cally felt hesitant, uncomfortable. She didn't want to make him feel sad again. But he'd brought the subject up.

"Yes, she did - just before she died." He paused.

Cally tried to frame in her mind the right thing to say. But he was talking again.

"She wrote me a letter. It said that the biggest thing in life to aim for was to have fun." He made a sound like a dry laugh. "Not so easy that... Not with her dying..."

Giles walked on ahead of her, his hands in his shorts' pockets, his head down. Cally felt a huge rush of sympathy. She noticed his towel had dropped off his shoulder onto the sand. "Hey, you dropped this," she shouted after him.

Giles stopped and turned.

She ran to catch up. "Thanks for telling me that," she said softly as she caught up. She dared to catch his gaze. "Your mom sounds really cool." Then she set off along the shoreline at a run. "Bet you can't catch me," she shouted.

Chapter

13

Thursday, Cally thought as she surfaced from sleep. Only three days of vacation left. But she only had to survive at school until Christmas. Then Cloverdale would be over, at least for the whole of next year. She turned on her side and thought back to her conversation with Giles. He was quite right, she thought, FUN was the ingredient missing from life at her present school. *Don't go there,* she thought. But it was too late. The memories were with her again. The agony of being laughed at for not being able to sing. She pulled the bedsheet over her head.

The last and worst occasion had to have been the debacle over the musical, *Mamma Mia,* the supposed highlight of the sixth-grade school year at Cloverdale, in its new-found role as an arts magnet school. Everyone in sixth grade was supposed to be involved in the production and music lessons were devoted to practice. Mrs. Snow must have known she couldn't sing, but she picked on her anyway. She'd made her try to sing the chorus to *Dancing Queen* on her own. How she hated that song. The rest of the class literally dissolved in laughter at her attempt, even when Mrs Snow told them to stop, even when they could surely see how red her face was and how she was only barely able to keep her shit together. And for weeks afterwards Tessa and Julia and Amy, her supposed buddies, would start singing stuff from *Mamma Mia*, just because they all had good roles in the performance of the musical. How come she couldn't be allowed to do math every day instead of music?

Cally gave an involuntary groan. That had been 6th grade at Cloverdale, and 7th grade wasn't shaping up to be much better.

I really do need to pee, Cally thought, brought back to the present by her bladder. She leapt out of bed. The moms were nowhere in sight. She bowed her head as she pulled down her PJs and sat on the toilet. She looked at herself in the mirror and used both hands to sweep her long, dark hair from her face. Who needed friends like that anyway?

She thought of Giles. Could he be a real friend? She felt that he was warming to her. But he was so moody and hard to read. Not surprising though, she thought, after what he'd endured in his life. Maybe a math focused school in Albany could be fun.

There was a loud knock on the door. She finished in the bathroom and ran to the door. She opened it to see Giles, his hand raised ready to bang again.

"Hey Cally, I thought you'd be up. Can I come in?"

Cally pulled the door wide and sat down on the edge of her mom's bed as Giles came in. He was dressed in jeans and a long sleeve adidas t-shirt, hair slicked back. He was clearly fresh out of the shower. He was carrying his laptop. He looked around.

"Beth and your mom at breakfast?"

"I guess so. I just got up."

"Great. So, I got a call from Petra." He sat down on the rickety chair that was a match to the one in his room, except that it had a sun-yellow cushion tied to the chair seat.

"What'd she say? Did they get good images?"

"We'll never know."

"What d'you mean?"

"So… she said that Shamus got into really deep shit from his boss. I guess the editor-in-chief or whatever you call it at his newspaper."

"What for?"

"Petra said that those white suited tanker-trailer guys from Tanglebell's reported him for flying the drone over their land. She said that Shamus thinks that his boss is being leaned on because Tanglebell has a lot of power around town, a big contributor to the paper or something. Anyway, he had the drone taken off him and he had to hand over the images file and everything he'd got. When he tried to object, and told the editor that there might be a link between the bad smell at the lake and Petra's mom's illness, his editor just told him he didn't have any evidence. So, he's been told to drop the story. He's really mad about it."

"Holy crap!"

"No kidding."

"So he can't write an article for the paper about the state of the lake and the pollution?"

"No." Giles shook his head. "Petra said Shamus wanted to quit his job, but he can't. He needs the money. Anyway, he's out of the picture."

"Aren't we supposed to have a free press? Didn't they teach us that in civics? What does Petra think?"

"She's really pissed. But not giving up. She's going to talk with people at the hospital and drive down to Augusta with the water samples today. She says it only takes 24 hours to get a preliminary analysis. But she said again that we should just leave it now. *We've done our bit*—her words exactly."

"That stinks." Cally felt angry. Everything had seemed so promising.

"Right, almost as much as the lake," said Giles.

Cally was surprised that he didn't sound very upset. She gave him a searching look.

"Well," he smiled, "I don't know about you, but I still have to get some photos to finish my project." He opened his laptop and turned the screen towards Cally. "Look, scroll through these. They're not good enough."

She took the laptop onto the bed and examined the photos.

"The oil drums in the dump one is fine, and so's the close-up of the water in the water bottle. But you're right, the others are crap. What we need is more evidence." Now she understood where he was going with this.

"So..." Giles grinned his green-eyed smile. "If the Penzance Post won't get involved..."

"What's the use of adults anyway?" Cally smiled.

"I guess it's up to us. Right partner?"

"And maybe we can find another way of getting the word out. There must be other papers in Maine." Cally suddenly felt hopeful.

He held up his hand and she slapped it. "We can do this," she said.

"But look, we've got to be careful. Not just because Beth and your mom will turn crazy if they find out what we've been doing, but..." Giles paused.

"Those guys are scary and maybe even dangerous?" said Cally.

"That too. And another thing, they're wearing those hazmat suits for a reason. That place is toxic."

"You're telling me. So, we'll be careful."

"Yeah, and I've been thinking. We've run into them three times now, and every time it's been in the morning. So, maybe we should go up this afternoon."

"But the moms are beginning to wonder what we're up to," said Cally.

"Beth's not my mom."

"Yeah, OK. But you know what I mean." Was he ever going to give up on that theme?

The door opened and Cally's mom came in followed by Beth.

"Hi, you two," her mom said. "Cally, what are you doing still in your PJs?"

Cally looked down. She'd been too occupied to even give her appearance a thought. But her mother didn't wait for a reply.

"Anyway, Beth and I have had an idea. It's going to be a lovely day. And the sea's completely calm. Why don't we rent some kayaks and paddle round the bay?"

Cally gave Giles a look as if to say *See what I mean?* But she had to admit the idea of kayaking did sound fun. She'd only ever canoed on a lake before. She looked at Giles. He shrugged.

"OK by me," said Giles.

"Me too," said Cally. "Bike ride tomorrow, then." After all, this was a vacation. The lake could wait a day.

Chapter

14

The *kayaks* turned out to be old, wooden two-person canoes. Aunt Beth rented them from a kiosk tucked in next to the pier on the bayside of the harbor. Cally shared a canoe with her aunt. For a little while it was fun to paddle between the shore and the pier. Even on this calm day the waves were much bigger than Cally had ever encountered on Lake Champlain. But after thirty minutes of going back and forth between the red buoy and the shore she was glad when Aunt Beth suggested heading back to the beach. They dragged the canoe out onto the warm sand and settled down on their towels. Aunt Beth slathered her pale legs with lotion as they watched the other two paddling across the bay. Giles was doing the lion's share of the work while her mom was leaning back, oar across her lap, apparently sunning herself.

"Janie always was the lazy one, even back when we were kids." Aunt Beth said.

"That's funny." Cally tried to imagine her mom as a child. She was the eldest of the three, with Aunt Beth the baby and Uncle Laurie the middle child and only boy. "Did she boss you around?"

"No, not much. She was always my protector. Laurie was such a nuisance brother to us both."

"It must have been nice to have a sister," Cally said.

"It was fun when we were small. Not so much when she was in high school though." Her aunt gave a little laugh, and smiled like a kid. "Janie's got quite a temper."

Cally nodded. She'd encountered her mom's temper from time to time.

"And I have to say she sometimes had good reason to be annoyed. I did keep taking her things," Aunt Beth admitted.

"What things?"

"Well, I remember this shell-covered jewelry box. I really loved it. It was lined with red velvet. But Janie being Janie, it wasn't full of jewelry. It contained her fossils and stones collection. She had amazing things in there, a fly trapped in amber, and shiny smooth rose-colored stones. I guess all scientists start out as collectors. Anyway, I used to *borrow* them. Aunt Beth made quotation marks in the air. "Janie did NOT appreciate that. But still we had some great times too." She paused, and looked over at Cally. "It must be lonely for you, and for Giles, being only kids."

Cally thought a moment. She definitely would have liked to have a sister, a real friend, but she wouldn't be cool with someone taking her prize possessions. "I guess it's just different," she said. "I mean, there's lots of little things, things that don't matter to grown-ups, that you don't get a chance to talk about…"

"Right. I think it's been really hard for Giles since his mom died."

Cally wondered how to ask her aunt about Giles. Obviously, she couldn't say *Giles doesn't like you.* She thought a minute and then said "Does he ever talk about her to you?"

Beth shook her head and looked down at the sand. "No, Giles and I…" she hesitated. "Well, we're still just getting to know each other." She turned to make eye contact before hurrying on. "Honest truth, Cally, I think he just resents me being around."

"Right, he's pretty moody."

"Because he's still mourning his own mom. He doesn't want me invading his space. It's pretty understandable."

Cally thought about that. "I guess that makes sense. I can see why that makes him sad."

"Yes, to see his dad with me and not his own mom. It's not surprising. Especially as his dad and I have so much in common, Ernest's job is writing books and mine's editing them, so we have to be careful not to spend all our time around him talking work. It's going to take a long time to become a family." Beth sighed.

"I think he wishes he could have stayed in his old house," Cally said.

"Did he say that?"

"Um, well, I don't remember his exact words… I guess it's all part of missing his mom."

"Maybe you're right. We thought he'd like my house because he has so much more space and its closer to his school. I've been wondering if that was the right move."

Beth seemed so sad. Cally felt an overwhelming need to cheer her up. She had always really liked her aunt. "Your house is great," she said. "I love visiting. And I'm glad his dad met you. I mean, you've given me a cousin." This was true. Since Cally's dad was an only child, and Uncle Laurie, her mom's brother, now lived in Spain with his wife and two-year-old twins she never saw, Giles was the only one anywhere near her age in the family.

"Thanks, Cally. You're the best." Her aunt smiled and patted the back of Cally's hand. "And at least Giles is clearly having a good time hanging out with you." She glanced out over the waves. "Hey look, they're on their way in. Let's go and help them out."

"Want to paddle over towards the lighthouse?" Cally asked Giles as she helped steady his canoe while her mother clambered out. The lighthouse stood out in red and white candy stripes and marked the southern-most edge of the cove. With the tide going out, the rocky out-crop on which it stood was edged with a yellow band of sand.

Giles looked over his shoulder in the direction she was pointing. "Sure," he said. "Climb aboard."

"Don't go too far away from the shore," her mom shouted as she waded away from them. "And come back soon."

"OK," she called. She clambered into her mom's seat at the front. See you soon." She picked up the paddle and tried to match her stroke to her cousin's. A few minutes later they were skirting the rocky shore heading towards the lighthouse.

"We need to get further out," Giles shouted.

He was right, the water was getting shallower, mak-ing it difficult to paddle. But Cally's attention had been drawn away from the water to the cliff face.

"Look," she said. "Look along the line of the cliffs." She pointed. "You can make out the hills we biked up." She moved her arm up and down, to make sure Giles was fol-lowing her gaze.

"Right," said Giles. "I'm kinda glad we're out here and not biking up there right now."

"Yeah. Me too," Cally agreed.

Giles stared towards the hills. Suddenly he stopped paddling.

"What's up?" she asked.

"I'm just thinking. That lake must drain somewhere, even if its fuller than when Petra was a kid. And water always runs off to lower ground, they drilled that into us in geography. So, what d'you think. Should we go check it out?"

"What? You mean see if there's oily water going down the cliff?"

"You got it."

"OK. Good job's the tide's out. I'm not planning to do any rock-climbing."

They plunged the oars in the water to make the prow of the canoe turn shore-wards. A few strokes later the canoe grounded.

They pulled it high onto the beach and Cally surveyed the view. The cliff face bulged in and out in folds marked by horizontal strata, first black at the base, then sandy brown in the middle, then pale grey below the line of green grass that marked the top. They threaded their way around rock pools at the base of the cliff.

"Looks pretty dry right here," Giles said, studying the cliff face. They went farther down the beach scrambling over rocks and jumping over rock pools. At one point, Cally almost lost her balance. Fighting to right herself, she looked down. The rock pool at her feet was similar to all the others, a ring of damp stones, a salt-water pond full of nooks and crannies, brown bladder wrack and green sea-grass lining its edges, but something was different. The surface of the water looked weird, like it had a sort of film on top. Cally knelt down and put her hand in the water. The liquid film parted.

"Look," she said, as she pulled her hand out. Both sides were coated in dark grey slime. "Gross." Cally rubbed her fingers and thumb together and felt them glide over each other. "It's oil."

Giles touched her hand. "Looks like it." He straightened up and gazed from the rock pool to the cliff face ahead. "And now I can see where it's coming from."

Cally followed his gaze. Several streams coursed through the sand towards the rockpool. They were coming from the cliff which was glistening with oily rivulets that ran down and splashed onto the beach in front.

"Look at that," he said. "It's disgusting. Talk about pollution…"

"And nobody knows about it."

They stood and stared.

"More evidence," said Cally.

"We need photos," he agreed. "I wish I'd brought my phone."

"Well, at least we can take some of these back with us,"

said Cally, picking up another sticky black rock. "We can show them to Petra."

"And we need some way of showing where we are in relation to the lake. I mean, I think it's up there, but I'm not certain," said Giles.

"Good point. I wish we had Shamus' drone." Cally cast her eyes out to sea, looking for a landmark that they might be able to see from the top of the cliff. "How about that black rock over there, the big one with the yellow one on top of it. It's shaped like a snowman."

"A snowman? You have to be kidding me."

"Well, there's a big and a small rock and they're two different colors and we should be able to recognize them again."

"OK. It's got a buoy on either side of it. That'll help."

"And the light-house is further off to the right. And if we can show that that oil came from the lake and is getting into the ocean," Cally rubbed the oil off Giles' hand, "That's important. That's got to get people interested."

"I suppose the alternative explanation is that the oil came from the ocean," Giles said.

"That wouldn't fit with the oil coming down the cliff, though." Cally glanced over at the black rivulets on the cliff face.

Giles nodded. "We can check online whether there's been any oil spills from tankers, just in case."

They collected several oily-slime covered rocks and headed back to the canoe.

"So, our last trip to Foggy Bottom tomorrow afternoon?" said Cally, as they pushed off.

"Sure thing," agreed Giles. "Let's work out a plan tomorrow morning."

The parents were waving to them on the beach as Cally and Giles paddled in towards the shore.

"Hold it," Giles said as he rammed his paddle in hard and back-stroked the canoe to a halt. He turned in his seat. "How are we going to explain these?" He pointed to the three oil-covered rocks rocking at the bottom of the boat.

"Good point." Cally looked over towards her mom and aunt. She thought a moment.

"How about we offer to paddle both canoes over to the rental? They've already paid for them, haven't they?"

"Right. OK, that should work. Here we go."

They paddled in the last few yards and Cally leapt out into the water. Giles hung back while she waded ashore.

"What on earth were you doing over there?" Cally's mom asked, clearly annoyed. "We've been waving at you to get over here for ages. The canoes were due back half an hour ago."

"I'm sorry. We didn't see you waving," Cally said,

which was true. "We were just looking at rock pools and there's some cool caves over there," which was also true.

Her mom sighed. "Come on then. Help me pull this one into the water. Let's get them over to the rental kiosk."

"We'll do it," Cally said quickly. "Giles and I can manage one each. You and Aunt Beth head back. I'll apologize to the rental guy."

"You sure?" Her mom seemed mollified by that idea.

Phew, thought Cally. She glanced back at Giles and risked a grin.

"Certain," he said. "No problem."

"OK, we'll go and get showered."

"I'm glad you two had a good time," said Aunt Beth. "Be quick. See you back at the hotel."

Giles nodded a half-smile, not at Cally, but at his aunt.

Wow! That's the first time I've seen him do that, Cally thought.

Chapter

15

Next morning, Cally and Giles had time to themselves while the parents investigated the antique shops of Penzance. They took up their usual stations in Giles' room. First Cally googled Tanglebell Oil and Gas company. The company seemed to have mining activities all over the US, according to the colorful map displayed online on their website. And their closest active location to Penzance was a mining area called Sandpiper about fifty miles away near the New Hampshire/Maine border.

"What do you make of this?" She read aloud:

"Tanglebell has generated the Sandpiper shale play, a new gas play on 85,000 acres. What's with the word *play?"*

"Wow," he said. "Shale play? I know what that is. It's where they extract natural gas. We had a lesson on it from this guy, this expert. He's the dad of one of my classmates, Theo Blane."

"That's cool." Cally said. "Another point in SAM's column."

"It actually WAS interesting," Giles said. "Did you know that the US leads the world in shale gas production?"

"You sound like an advert for gas companies!"

"But listen," Giles leapt off the bed. "Getting the gas out uses loads and loads of water. They push it down into the ground using massive pressure to force the gas up. It's called fracking. It produces masses of waste liquid. I'll bet you that's what they're pumping into the lake."

"But dumping water wouldn't cause that mess," she said. "It's got to be the stuff leaking from those drums."

"Right," Giles agreed. "They're definitely exhibit A, but the fluid from fracking, it's toxic too."

Giles dove back onto his bed and grabbed his laptop. "He gave us this essay to read. I'll see if I can google it."

Seconds later, he was up again.

"Look, read this. It's in *Scientific American.*" Giles read out the title, *"Fracking can contaminate drinking water."*

Given that title, Cally was eager to read on*. It actually said that fracking fluid contained all sorts of chemicals and gases, things that can cause cancer and can affect people's nervous systems.

"You might be right," she said. "It could definitely be a combination of things." And maybe it could leak into Petra's mom's well water, she thought. The waters all

---

*https://www.scientificamerican.com/article/fracking-can-contaminate-drinking-water/

smelled the same. She realized that she'd never given much thought to where drinking water came from. Any school had to be better than Cloverdale at teaching geography, she thought. Giles was deep in his screen again.

"Giles, how do you think toxic stuff could get to Moms' house?"

"I was just looking into that," he said. "The water in wells comes from ground-water and that's in contact with lakes and streams as well as the stuff that rains down. And her house is definitely down the hill from the lake and the quarry. It's like this."

He grabbed the piece of hotel stationary on the rickety desk and the tiny pencil that accompanied it, and drew a sketch of the quarry, the lake and the cliff. Then he added the road going down to Penzance.

"And Moms' house is down here between the road and the lake." Cally said, jabbing a point on the map.

"Right. I'll tart this sketch up for my homework project. We just need more proof. We don't even know for certain that the water from the quarry stream goes down that pipe into the lake. How can we prove that?"

Cally stared at the wall over the top of her laptop, thinking hard, while Giles continued to tap frantically on his screen.

"Look," he said. "Geography is on our side."

She leaned over and saw that he'd pulled up a website

The map that Giles prepared for his homework

that showed contour maps from every state. Who knew geography could be so cool? She watched him zoom into the area around Penzance on the map of Maine, find Foggy Bottom, the *gravel pit* with the stream in it and all the contour lines around them.

"See? This is the cliff we climbed up. Look, it's almost eighty feet up." He marked that height on the sketch.

Cally noticed how close the contour lines were. "Wow. We got up there?"

"Yep. And the lake's at around the one hundred contour line," he said. "And the waste pit is at one hundred and twenty feet, and water always travels downhill."

"But how to prove it?" Cally persisted. "Listen, I have an idea. What If we had a load of red colored dye, we could put it in the stream at the pipe, and see it emerge into the lake?"

"Nah. Where would we get enough dye by this afternoon?" Giles said. He started to scroll through the photos he had taken of the quarry area. Cally watched over his shoulder.

"I know," he said, his voice triumphant.

"What?" asked Cally.

"That—the weeds—the goldenrod." He stabbed at the screen for emphasis. "We can pick a load of it, dump it in the stream. It floats and it's easy to spot. That's what we can use."

That afternoon, fueled by a large brunch of pancakes, Maine blueberries, maple syrup and melted butter, Cally and Giles pedaled uphill.

"All right, let's do it!" Giles shouted ahead of her.

He'd reached the No Trespassing sign at the top of the hill, but he did not stop. They'd agreed that his first mission was to cycle on down the road to the gate where they'd encountered the Tanglebell tanker trailer the last time. They needed to know that there was no one parked up there, no one to catch them. Meanwhile, Cally got off her bike at the usual place, hid the bike in the bushes out of sight from the road and carefully laid the orange jacket over the barbed wire.

"All clear," announced Giles as he rode up, breathless. "No sign of anyone."

They were over the stone wall in seconds, Cally leading the way this time. The route through the woods was by now easy to find, marked as it was by trodden down vegetation. They ran along it until they reached the path between the waste quarry and Foggy Bottom. As they emerged from the woods the sun disappeared behind a cloud and the wind picked up. Cally felt like she was being blown along like a kite. The hood of her hoodie slammed into the back of her head and her hair whipped in her face.

"Maybe the wind will blow the fog away from the lake," she shouted to Giles as he came up behind her.

"Fingers crossed," said Giles.

Round one more bend and down the hill, Cally thought. Then she broke into a run.

"It's Non-Foggy Bottom!" she shouted from the crest of the hill. They looked down over the wide-expanse of water. The wind whipped the surface into shimmering waves, and the trees on the far side bent in unison with each gust.

"Perfect," said Giles. "But first let's go over to the cliff and see if we can see your snowman rock."

They headed on to the edge of the cliff, to the point where they had emerged after they'd escaped the incoming tide on their first day here. The wind was even stronger here. They looked down over the precipice and out to sea. Giles put his hand on Cally's shoulder, as a gust threatened to blow her over the edge.

"Look! That's it," she shouted. It was the presence of the two red buoys that helped her to spot it. Once she saw them and aligned them with the lighthouse in the distance, she concentrated on the rock that lay between. It was roiled by waves, brought alive by spray. But it was undoubtedly her double-barreled snowman rock. As they watched, a large wave crashed over its head and water cascaded off its giant nose.

"You're right. The oil on the beach must be just down there." Giles pulled off his backpack, dug around in it and pulled out a small black camera. "Let's get a picture so we can show Petra where to look."

They had borrowed Cally's mom's point and shoot camera, on the pretext of getting holiday snapshots. Cally had used it before and knew that its big range of focus made for much better photos than they could get with Giles' phone. Not that the pictures they were planning to get were the sort of photos her mom was expecting. But this had not been exactly the beach holiday that Cally had been expecting either.

"OK, on to Plan B," said Giles as he stashed the camera away again in the backpack. "Here, you take the backpack to keep the camera dry."

"Right, we'd better be quick. That looks like real rain coming."

Cally pointed behind them. A large bank of blue-black cloud was advancing towards them from the west.

They split up, Giles to go to the waste dump to cut bunches of goldenrod with his pocket knife, and throw them into the pipe. Cally's role was to climb down to the lake and see if she could spot any of the weeds appearing in the water. She would take photos, climb back out and they'd meet up back at the stone wall.

"Remember, give me about ten minutes," Giles said.

"At most fifteen. If you haven't seen anything by then, just get pictures of the dead fish and scram."

"OK." Cally checked her watch. 3.07pm. "I'll see you back at the wall. I'll be there by three-thirty. Good luck."

Cally was glad that she'd worn jeans as she made her way down the steep side of the slope. No way was she going to fall this time, she thought. She scrambled along, sliding much of the time on the seat of her pants. The backpack bounced up and down on her back. The wind died down as soon as she started her descent, but its noise was replaced by her breath, and falling shale that she dislodged as she slid. It wasn't until she reached the bottom that she could take in the scene.

Cally gazed around. Good to be here on my own, she thought. It was so much easier to concentrate. She was going to work this scene like a detective. At first glance it looked like a snapshot from a dream vacation, beautiful Maine countryside, a broad expanse of water, edged with hills forested with sumac, pines and oak. Until you noticed that the trees nearest to the water's edge had the bottom of their trunks submerged, and that their branches were devoid of fall leaves. And the smell…

She took a full breath in. Was it as stinky as before? She closed her eyes and took several deep breaths. The smell was so bad it felt like it dissolved into a bad taste at the back of her throat. Burnt eggs laced with sweetly sweaty socks. It was definitely still there, even on this windy day. She had not imagined it.

She took off her backpack and looked into the view finder of her mom's camera, a landscape scene that captured the drowned trees. She clicked the shutter button and checked the recorded image. Looks good, she thought. First goal achieved.

Next the water. You really would expect the water here not to be polluted, she thought. It should be crystal clear. It's supposed to be pretty. And it isn't. Slate grey sludge marked the water's edge on the rocks. She followed the shore a little way, looking for the shoal of fish. It was difficult to keep from slipping because of the slime, but she wanted to get a shot of the dead fish for the records.

When she found them, the ragged, floating forms were virtually unrecognizable, just grey scraps of tissue and fragments of silvery scales, and one recognizable fish tail. Nobody's going to believe they're fish, she thought. She snapped some shots, then remembered that she was supposed to be checking for goldenrod. She checked her watch, 3.16pm, and looked over the lake a third time. No sign of any yellow weed. But she'd better be ready. She sat down on a boulder and waited.

A sound caught her attention, the *mew, mew, kew* of a seagull. It had been there in the background since the beginning of her climb down, and she'd paid no attention to it. After all, you'd expect to hear seagulls. But now she realized the bird must be very close by, and it was making a lot of noise.

Mew, mew, keoooow, mew, mew, keooow.

She stood up, camera in hand, just in case the goldenrod should appear and moved towards the bird-call. It was coming from behind a small pile of sand, rock and marram grass.

Cally stopped dead as the gull came into view. The black pupil of its pale blue eye stared straight back at her. Its body lay on its side, only the head and one wing making any attempt at movement. The wing was outstretched, its feathers plastered together with blue-black oil. Its tail and back feathers were also oiled, in stark contrast to the white of its neck and head, and its long, yellow beak was stained along its length as if dipped in ink. *Keoow, keoow* it cried again and dug its beak into its damaged wing.

The bird made no attempt to move away as Cally took pictures. "You poor thing," she murmured as she worked. She wondered if she should try to catch it. Could she try to clean it up somehow? She moved closer, hand outstretched, almost close enough to touch...

Its neck shot out, beak open, ready to peck.

"OK, OK," she said. "I guess I can't help." Anyway, I've got to concentrate on the goldenrod, she thought. She scanned the lake. There was still no sign of any on the water.

A sudden thought occurred to her. Maybe she should have been looking from the top of the cliff? She'd have been able to see further. Cally felt stupid. It was already 3.20. Giles had had thirteen minutes to grab weeds and throw them down the pipe.

Oh God! I shouldn't have climbed down; I should have stayed up top, she thought. She ran back to the rucksack and started the climb back up.

By 3.25 she reached the path, and her chest was heaving. She turned toward the lake and stared down. A rivulet of gold spread out across the water.

"Yeahhh!" she screamed, and bent down to retrieve the camera.

"Hey!" A loud voice cried. A shout that died away in the wind. An angry voice. Where was it? Behind her? Towards the cliff? One thing Cally knew for certain. It was not Giles' voice.

She froze.

"Hey, you there."

The voice was closer.

She forced herself not to look round. *Concentrate, take a picture. Just get the picture, NOW,* she commanded herself. She willed herself to focus, first on the camera, then the water, then the band of yellow. I have to get the picture. Do not look round. The camera clicked.

"Hey, STOP THAT!" Closer still.

She pushed the camera back in the backpack and turned. Two figures, two figures in white were heading towards her. Cally broke into a run.

Chapter

16

Blood pounded in her head as she raced up the trail. The wind was in her face. She couldn't tell whether her pursuers were gaining on her. But she knew they were there—panting, shouting, pounding towards her. A rumble of thunder echoed overhead. She turned a corner and realized she was close to where their trail led back to the barbed-wire fence.

If I can just get to the turnoff before they make it around this corner, she thought. She put on a spurt, imagined the corner as a finish line of a race and flew. She made it to the turnoff. Her lungs were bursting. She prayed that Giles was already back at the meeting place. She could see the top of the barbed wire fence ahead. No sign of Giles. Was he over the other side of the wall? She didn't dare shout in case the men were still behind. One final push and she was climbing the wall. The anorak was still there. No sign of Giles.

From the top of the wall Cally scanned frantically around. Still no Giles. Where was he? Still at the waste dump? Hiding from the men, maybe. They must have kept on the main path, not seen her turn off. She took a deep breath. As long as they hadn't seen Giles, it was going to be OK. She just had to wait. She grabbed the anorak off the barbed wire, just in case they caught a glimpse of its orange, rolled it in a ball, hugged it to herself and sat leaning back against the stone wall. Drops of rain the size of ice hockey pucks began to splash on her head. It was already 3.40. Where was Giles?

Five minutes passed. The rain was coming down in a continuous sheet. Another roll of thunder made the world shudder.

Ten minutes passed. Still no sign of Giles. Surely the Tanglebell men would have gone by now? They'd surely have given up searching and wanted to shelter from the rain. So, what was he doing? Had they caught him? Cally felt fear welling up inside. It was as if a cold hand was constricting her throat. Her heart raced. Think, she commanded herself.

He wouldn't leave without me. I know that. So, he's at the waste dump. So, I have to find him. Best to do it while it's still raining.

She stood up and shivered. No point putting the anorak on. Its color was like a beacon for anyone looking.

She put it in the backpack and slung that over her shoulders to leave her arms free.

Cally retraced her steps back to the main path between Foggy Bottom and the quarry. She didn't want to run in case the Tanglebell men were still around. She wanted to see them before they saw her. Rain dripped down in a steady stream, and the clouds were so dark it seemed like dusk. Now that she was away from the shelter of the trees and the wall, the wind was biting cold. She reached the quarry and slid down on her backside. She barely noticed the spray of water around her as she descended. Why had he not come? Could they really have got him?

No, she thought. He's got to be hiding. She reached the bottom. In the shelter of the quarry walls it was eerily quiet, as wet as a cave. *He has to be here.* The oil drums looked massive in the gloom, dank and dripping. The goldenrod, the goldenrod! It was trodden down in some places, broken off in others. She knew he'd put the weeds in the pipe. She'd seen them on the other side. She turned towards the stream. It was more like a raging torrent.

"Cally! Over here!"

Cally's heart leapt. Never had she been so relieved to hear a voice. Giles' head poked out from behind an oil drum that was propped against the quarry wall. She smiled with relief to see his dirt-streaked face and bedraggled hair.

"Giles," she shouted and splashed through puddles towards him. "Why didn't you come?"

"I couldn't." He hopped towards her, using the oil drum for support. "My ankle." He was holding his left leg bent at the knee, his foot off the ground. "Are they gone?"

She reached him and had to suppress the huge urge to give him a hug. The set of his lips and rigidity of his body told her that he was in no mood for affection. He was in real pain. "What happened?" she asked. "Did they chase you too?"

"Nah. But I heard them screaming at you. You were on the path back from Foggy Bottom, weren't you?" He slid down onto his butt into the mud in front of her, with his back against the oil drum. The rain had eased off to a gentle drizzle and the drum offered some shelter from the wind. Cally settled down beside him.

"Yeah. But I got ahead of them and made it over the wall." She glanced down at his left foot. "I waited for you, but now I know why you didn't come." She pointed to his ankle. "How bad is it?"

"Pretty bad. I can't stand on it. I couldn't climb up the side of the quarry. I've tried."

She followed his gaze down to his hands. His fingers and nails were caked with mud and his palms were streaked with blood.

"Oww, those must hurt," she said. "How did it happen?"

"So, like I said, I heard them following you. It was like a herd of buffalo stampeding. I was coming back up along the stream over there." He pointed towards where the stream disappeared into the pipe. "So I started running. I knew I needed to get somewhere they couldn't see me. And it was tipping down and all the rocks were slippery and I put all my weight on one to put up a sprint and then the rock moved and my foot slipped and my ankle, my ankle..." he stopped and took a breath. Cally realized he was stopping himself from crying. "Then I felt really bad, sick and dizzy, and so I couldn't get up and I just lay down in the grass and the weeds for a bit. And then I waited and waited and then I tried to climb out, and I couldn't. God, I wished you had a phone..." his voice trailed off.

"Tell me about it. I thought of that too. But there's no service down here, remember? So, it wouldn't have made a difference."

"Right," Giles nodded. He winced as he readjusted the position of his foot. "Anyway, I figured that if you'd got away you'd eventually come looking for me and this was about the driest place to wait. Then I heard someone climbing down, and I thought it'd be you, but I hid round the other side just in case." Giles looked down at the backpack Cally was cradling in her lap. "So, did you see it? The goldenrod?"

"Yeahh. Christ I'd almost forgotten. It worked like a dream. I think I got good photos. I kept the camera dry." She patted the backpack.

"Great."

Cally saw the weak smile on Giles' face. He made no move to get up. It was as if a heavy wet blanket was holding him down. One look at him made her realize there was no way he was going to climb out of the quarry, with or without her assistance. And they were definitely not going to be riding the bikes.

"Look, it's stopped raining. We've got to get out of here," she said. "I'll take your phone and call the moms. I can get enough signal at the top of the quarry."

"For Christ's sake, not them. They'll go apeshit. And they don't know where we are anyway. Call Petra."

Cally thought about that. She was pretty sure their parents were going to go apeshit whatever happened. But maybe Giles did have a point. If Petra gave them a ride back to the hotel there'd be less explaining to do. Maybe Petra could enlist Shamus' help? How else were they going to get Giles up the side of the quarry? "OK," she said. "Petra first. But if she's not answering it'll have to be my mom."

"Deal," he agreed. He dug the phone out of the back-pocket of his jeans and handed it to her. "The password's *shitshow*. Be quick."

Cally needed no encouragement. She left the back-pack with Giles and raced around the oil drums and pools of dank water to the quarry side. Shit-show, shit-show, shit-show she said to herself as she climbed, her heart pounding. The soaked surface gave her no traction so she resorted to moving upwards on all-fours, grab-bing like a monkey on roots and rocks as she went. She gasped for air as she reached the top. "Shitshow," she said as she pulled out the phone and keyed in the password. She scrolled through his call log, and dialed Petra.

"Hey Giles, what's up?"

"It's not Giles, it's me," Cally panted, still short of breath.

"Hey, Cally. Are you OK? I've just walked into your hotel. I'm standing here chatting with your mom."

Shit, thought Cally. Busted. "OK," she said, "we need help."

Chapter

17

Cally was amazed at Shamus' strength, as he carried Giles piggy-back style up the steep incline from the quarry. She watched from above as Beth and her mom clucked behind him like chicks around a mother hen, until first one then the other slipped and had to turn their attention to their own feet. Then the walk back to the road took forever, with Shamus and Aunt Beth acting as crutches supporting Giles' weight as best they could. By the time they'd helped him over the barbed wire fence, his face was sickly pale, except for the streaks of oil that smeared one side. He hopped the last few steps to the pick-up truck and Petra ran ahead to open the doors. Cally held her mom's hand as she gingerly climbed over the wall. She saw her mom gaze at the NO TRESPASSING sign as they moved away. They made eye contact. No humor there.

"Later," was all her mother said.

As she jumped down, Cally remembered the hotel bikes. She ran towards their hiding place.

"Mom, can you give me a hand?" she called. "The bikes are here."

Cally hauled on the sit-up-and-beg handlebars of one of them and pushed it towards the back of Shamus' truck. Her mother followed her example and Shamus came around to load them into the back.

"We should take him for an X-ray," he said. "There's a walk-in clinic about a 5-minute drive from your hotel. Beth and I'll take him over there."

Beth nodded her agreement. They'd obviously been discussing this.

"I'll ride back with you, shall I?" Petra asked, turning to Cally's mom. Giles had already stretched out on the backseat of the truck.

"Of course," said Cally's mom. "I'll drop you at your home."

"Great; it's not far from your hotel."

As her mother climbed into the driver's seat and closed the door, Petra hung back. She pulled on Cally's arm, stopping her from getting into the car.

"Why on earth did you come back?" she whispered.

"To get photos," Cally explained. "What did you tell Mom?"

"Not much. That I knew where you were, that you'd

been exploring Foggy Bottom. I'd only just got to the ho-tel when you called. There wasn't time for explanations. They just raced upstairs to get their car keys and followed me and Shamus up here."

"Right, but ..."

Shamus' truck pulled away down the road. Cally's mom opened the passenger side window and leaned over. "Come on, you two. I need you out of those wet things Cally. We can talk later."

The laminated card in the shower read: *Please conserve water; limit your shower to 5 minutes.* Cally knew that at least ten minutes must have passed. Her head was turned up towards the shower head. The hot water streaming over her face felt good. She closed her eyes and tried to imagine herself telling the story to her mom. That was going to be the next challenge. Her mom's words, as she'd handed her a fresh towel and some dry clothes and pointed to the bathroom, had been "Shower, get dry and then we talk. OK?"

Yes, she thought, this is going to be OK. After all, their only crime had been trespassing, and once Mom under-stood why they'd been at Foggy Bottom, could she really be annoyed? As long as Giles was OK...

She turned off the shower and heard a knock on the bathroom door. "Are you ever coming out?"

"Almost ready," she shouted. She toweled and put on the sweats and thick socks her mom had provided.

"Good news," her mom said as Cally walked back into their bedroom. "Beth called. Giles has torn ligaments but no bones broken. They're fitting him for crutches."

Cally stood still. She felt tears of relief well up. Before she could stop herself, she was crying. And the next thing she knew her mother was there, enclosing her in warmth. She cried into that safe space.

"It's OK; it's OK." Her mom's soft voice, like the silky edge of a security blanket. Finally, the wave passed. Cally lifted her head.

"Thanks," she said, her voice thick through a blocked nose. "I'm sorry we worried you."

"That's alright. Here." Her mom reached for the box of tissues on the bedside table.

Cally sat down on the edge of the bed and blew her nose.

"Do you want to start from the beginning?" her mom asked as she sat back into the cushions of the one easy chair in the room.

"OK." Cally took a deep breath and thought back to the beginning of the week. "So, you remember the fog on Monday?" she started.

Her mother nodded, as she settled into the chair.

Cally described the walk up the beach through the rock pools, the tide coming in, the climb up the cliff.

"My God!" her mom interjected. "You could have died. And you didn't tell us?"

"It wasn't that dangerous," Cally said hastily. "Anyway, that's how we ended up at the lake, Foggy Bottom, in the first place. We didn't know we were trespassing."

"OK. So, Petra said that the lake is polluted, by stuff coming from that quarry? The place where we found Giles today?"

"That's right." Cally felt her mom's interest. Maybe her scientist's curiosity might outweigh her annoyance, she hoped. She hurried on. "And Giles wanted to write about the pollution for his school science homework. That's why we went back there today. We wanted to get pictures. And that's why we borrowed your camera. And I got some good ones I think." She glanced over at Giles' backpack. It was still lying on the floor by the door where she'd dropped it. "I can show you," she said.

Cally was on her feet and opening the backpack before her mother could reply. The camera was still tucked in the inside-pocket, dry as a bone. She pressed the play-back button and scrolled through. "Yes," she said with relief. The photos were all there, clear, in focus, perfect.

Her mother came over and perched on the side of the bed next to her.

"So, that's what the lake looks like from a distance," she said, showing her mother the first frame. "Pretty beautiful, you'd think."

Her mom regarded the screen. "Right. Gorgeous. That's some black cloud on the horizon though."

"But when you zoom in you see this…" She showed her mother a frame that was a close up of the oily scum on the water's surface, and then the pictures of the dead fish.

"Gross," her mom said.

"And the smell, you wouldn't believe how bad it smells," she added. "It gave me a headache."

"I could smell it at the quarry too," her mom said. "It WAS gross. Anyway, how did Petra and Shamus get involved?" her mom asked. "I thought they were taking you sight-seeing on Wednesday. Instead you went to this stinky, oily lake?"

"Well yes. But it wasn't like that. It was because of Petra's mom. When we were walking back from Foggy Bottom that first day, we found her, remember? Well, her dog found us to be exact."

Her mom nodded.

"And the smell in her house was just like the smell of the water at the lake," Cally continued. "And on Tuesday, Giles and I got samples of the lake and quarry water and we met Petra by chance at her mom's house. So, Petra

took the samples and her mom's water sample to get tested at the state lab in Augusta, to see if there was something toxic that caused her mom to collapse."

"Hold on. Slow down." Cally's mom leaned forward
in her chair. "How could that be? Is her house near the
lake?"

"Yes, not far. They have well water, just like we have.
And they're down the hill from the lake, we checked on a
map online. And we did some research this morning and
it's true that the ground water that our water wells tap
into is also connected to lakes and rivers isn't it?

"Sure, otherwise in dry weather lakes and rivers would
dry up completely," her mom agreed. "So Petra thought it
was worth testing?"

"Right. And Shamus was going to write a story about
the pollution for the Penzance Post. You know that that's
his job, he's a reporter?"

"No, you didn't tell me," she said pointedly.

"Well anyway, his boss wouldn't let him write it."

"Why ever not? Surely that would make a good article
for the local paper. If I lived here I'd want to know."

"Petra said that the editor said there was no evidence."

"I thought reporters' jobs were to get evidence." Cally's mom said dryly. "Anyway, that explains why Shamus
and Petra knew where to find you two today. You went

with them on Wednesday when you were supposedly being shown around Penzance?"

"Yes, but they did take us for ice cream too," Cally added. She hurried on before her mother could ask more about that. "Petra used to play there as a kid. She remembers it was clean back then."

"So who's polluting the area now?"

"It's owned by an oil and gas company. Giles and I did some research on them for his project. It's called Tanglebell. Here." Cally typed in the name on her laptop and showed her mother the page she'd browsed earlier.

Her mom scrolled down the page. "OK. So, they own it; but there's laws about groundwater pollution." She paused, seeming to gather her thoughts, then sat back, her face serious. "You could have told us, you know, me and Beth. What you were doing. You basically lied."

Cally felt her face flush but she plunged on. "You'd have stopped us. You wouldn't even let me walk in the fog on my own." She didn't want to admit that half the fun for both her and Giles had been keeping the parents in the dark.

"And you knew you were trespassing?"

"Yes," she mumbled. "But..." Cally paused. Whatever she said was going to make matters worse, she thought.

"And you still haven't explained how Giles twisted his ankle." Her mom gave Cally a hard stare. "Were you really just running for shelter from the storm?"

That had been the quick explanation she and Giles had concocted as they'd waited for help to come to get out of the quarry. But what really was the point in lying?

"No," she said in a rush. "These men from Tanglebell saw me and shouted at me and started to chase me and we both ended up running and it was raining really hard and that's how he fell." She stopped, held her breath and looked her mother in the eye. "That's the truth. And I'm really sorry, Mom. But..."

"Enough." Her mom was on her feet. She shook her head in exasperation and started to pace. The tension in the room rose with each step.

"Bee-dupp, bee-dupp..."

The noise of her mother's ring tone broke the silence. Her mom retrieved her cell phone from the bedside table and swiped the screen.

"Hi Petra," she said, nodding into the phone. "Yes, he's OK. Beth called to tell me. He's got a bad sprain but nothing broken." She looked across at Cally. "Yes, she's here. OK."

She handed the phone to Cally. "Petra wants to speak to you."

"Hi Petra."

"Hi Cally. So glad Giles is OK."

"Me too."

"Look, we need to talk. I got the first test results. And there's definitely toxic things in the water. That was what I was gonna tell you when I went to the hotel. But then with Giles' fall and everything..." She paused. "Anyway, it can wait till tomorrow. Do you think we can get together then?"

"I think so. We're not leaving till Sunday. I'll just check with my mom." Cally glanced over to her mother. "Petra's got the test results about the water. She wants to show me and Giles tomorrow. Is that OK?"

"As long as Beth and I are there too."

"OK." Cally knew there was no point arguing.

"And we'd better meet up here," her mother added. "Giles is not going to be going far on crutches."

Cally turned back to the phone. "Sure. Can you come over to the hotel?"

"Coffee time?" suggested her mother.

"OK. 10 o'clock in the restaurant. See you then."

It wasn't until later that evening that Cally had a chance to talk to Giles in private. She and her mom had collected Giles and Aunt Beth from the walk-in clinic, and then the whole story had to be gone through again for Beth's benefit over dinner. The sisters had finally adjourned to the bar for a *well-earned drink,* to finish off what had been for them *a trying day.*

Cally knocked on Giles' bedroom door and then realized that it might be tricky for him to open it. She tried the handle and the door swung open.

Giles was sitting up against the headboard of his bed, his crutches propped up on one side. "Come in," he said.

"I brought your backpack," she said dropping it on the floor.

"Great. Do you still have your mom's camera?"

Cally held up her hand. "Yep."

"Let's put our pictures together. And we should add in the websites of the *Scientific American* article and the contour map. Then we can leave a copy with Petra." Giles reached for his laptop that was stationed by his side on the bed. "Mine are already on here. Let's have the memory card." Cally took the chip from the camera and handed it over.

"Let's see," he said as he loaded it up and browsed the row of pictures that had appeared on the screen. "Wow, Cally, these are pretty good! Especially this one." He turned the screen around to show her the shot of the oil-covered seagull.

"It was right near where we saw those dead fish," she said. "It was so awful. It kept burying its beak into its wing, trying to get the oil off and cawing like it was being tortured. I really wanted to help it but I couldn't think how," she said. "It tried to peck me when I got any closer."

"And this, your pic of the goldenrod in the lake, it's great. It even looks like the weeds are fanning out from a single source, where they came through the pipe."

"I took that one literally while the Tanglebell men were barreling up the path screaming at me like I was a murderer," Cally said. "It's a miracle it came out." She didn't even try to keep the pride out of her voice.

Giles grinned. "OK, OK, super-girl. You did OK, right?" He handed her back the memory chip. "Now, leave me in peace while I put this lot together."

"OK, OK, peg leg. Mom told me not to pester you." Cally got up to leave. She paused at the door. "I'm glad it's not broken," she said.

Back in her shared bedroom, Cally settled down on her own bed. Her legs felt sore from the exertions of the day.

What a day, she thought. But despite Giles' fall and the tricky talk she'd had with her mom, she felt content. After all, they had achieved what they had set out to do. She smiled at the thought of Giles calling her super-girl. She'd be sad when they parted company tomorrow.

That thought brought back to mind the other purpose of this trip. So, what about Singapore? It was time for a decision. Her thoughts drifted between the future and the past, times experienced, unknowns to come. As she mused, the germ of an idea formed. *I wonder*, she thought, and sat up. "Need to talk to Dad," she said out loud, and reached for her laptop.

Chapter

18

The last day, Cally thought as she walked into the dining room, better make the most of it. The morning sun flooded in through the bay window that overlooked the parking lot. Her mom, Aunt Beth and Giles had taken over the one big circular table in the center of the room, and the only other occupants were two grey-haired retirees nestled in a corner immersed in their newspapers. The waitress, who Cally knew also worked as a receptionist some evenings, was pouring coffee into white mugs. Giles was tucking into a muffin, his injured ankle stretched out in front of him encased in a large grey moon boot.

Her mom looked up as she walked over to the table. "Quick Cally. They're going to stop serving any minute. What do you want?" she asked.

"One of those," she said, pointing to Giles' muffin. "And some OJ, please."

She glanced into the parking lot as she sat down, to see a familiar green pick-up truck pulling into a space. "Looks like Petra's here," she said, "and Shamus too."

"OK, let's order some coffee for them both," said her mom. "Shift up a bit Cally, so there's room for them to sit."

A few minutes later Petra bounced into the room followed at a more leisurely pace by Shamus. Petra wore a bright yellow t-shirt, a waistcoat that matched her bangs in color and distressed-looking denims. Her ruby red smile flashed energy like a solar flare.

"So great to see you," she said, as she made her way around the table to shake hands with her mom and Beth. She looked down at Giles' outstretched leg. "How's the ankle?"

"It's fine," said Giles, waving at his foot. "Can't feel a thing in there. The crutches are a pain though."

"I'll bet. That happened to me a couple of winters ago, except it was my knee. I slipped on the ice outside my apartment and next thing I knew, WHOP, down on my chin…"

Shamus pulled Petra down into a seat and plopped a ring-bound notebook down in the space in front of him.

"Good to see you both, too," said Cally's mom. "We ordered you coffee. Is that OK?"

"Sure," said Shamus as he wriggled out of his tartan-lined jacket.

"Thanks, but I'll change it to OJ if that's OK," said Petra. "Not a coffee person."

Petra caught the eye of the server and changed her order.

"How's your mom, Petra?" Beth asked.

"She's doing much better. Going to be discharged today. I'm collecting her this afternoon. But the big news is..." Petra paused and looked around the table. All eyes were on her. "Well, this is what I wanted to tell you yesterday. Before everything happened. That's why I came over here to find you. My friend at the lab in Augusta called with the preliminary test results on the water and it turns out that Moms really, really does have bad water and the lake water is even worse, and the quarry water is the worst. And what's more they've got the same contaminant." She breathed out and turned to Shamus. "What was it called?"

"I put it in here somewhere," he muttered as he leafed through the pages of his notebook. "Here it is."

He unfolded a sheet of paper and started to read. "According to the lab, the water from Foggy Bottom and the quarry and the sample from Petra's moms' faucet, all contain above normal levels of benzene."

"What's that?" asked Cally.

"That's bad," her mom said with emphasis. Cally glanced over at her mother. She had the intense look on her face that Cally recognized, the look that said, I am in work mode, the scientist not the mom.

"Right," agreed Shamus. "I looked it up too." He continued reading from his notes. *"Benzene contamination in well water can result from leakage of petroleum products from waste storage sites."* He looked up. "It's the stuff that gas stations smell of. *And benzene can cause drowsiness, dizziness, irregular heart beat and headaches."*

"She also said that the quarry water bottle smelled of hydrogen sulfide," added Petra. "It's the gas that smells like bad eggs. And that's what Foggy Bottom and Moms' house smells like. But they don't have a good quick test for hydrogen sulfide. It evaporates very quickly. They're going to do a lot more testing."

"WOW," Cally put down her glass of orange juice.

"No shit!" said Giles.

"Giles!" Aunt Beth looked at him.

"Sorry, but that's just made me an A grade for my project!" he said.

"This is not funny." Cally's mom's voice broke through the notes of celebration. "You guys have been up at this lake exposed to this stuff every day this week. And Petra's mom may have collapsed because of it." She stared hard at Cally, "I'm not happy about how you've gone about this but I do think you've found out something that's really important." Her face broke into a half-smile that lit up her eyes and wrinkled her brow.

Cally breathed a sigh of relief. She smiled back at her mother.

Petra nodded her agreement, but for once it was Shamus who spoke first.

"Agreed. As soon as Petra told me this I took it to my boss. Did Cally and Giles tell you I work for the Penzance Post?"

Cally's mom nodded.

"Janie told me," said Beth.

"Well, so the editor-in-chief, he's called Mr. Bullock. He'd stopped me from investigating *Tanglebell.* But I told him the lab result, and now he's given me the green-light to follow up on it. I can write an article for the paper."

"Fantastic," said Cally.

"That's the right thing to happen," agreed her mom. Cally noticed that the set of her shoulders had relaxed a little.

"We've got great photos you can use," said Giles. "Do you want to see the PowerPoint I made? Beth, do you have my laptop?"

"Here you are." Aunt Beth slid the computer over to Giles.

Giles opened the laptop and found the PowerPoint, while everyone tried to arrange themselves to be able to see the screen.

"This isn't going to work," said Giles. His boot-covered foot could not fit under the table so it was impossible for people to gather round him. "Here, you go through it with them, Cally," he said. "I'll listen."

And so Cally did. First came the pictures of the rusted, leaking oil-drums at the waste dump and the rainbow swirls of color of the oil-film in the stream. Next Giles had inserted a picture of the goldenrod where he'd thrown it into the stream, at the spot where the pipe disappeared into the hillside.

"Why did you take pictures of that?" asked Beth.

"It's the evidence we needed," Giles explained. We put the weeds in the stream to see if they'd come out into the lake, and they did. So toxic stuff in the stream does get into the lake."

"Right. But we're not just worried about the oil drums." Petra said. Beth and Cally's mom both looked up from the screen.

"What d'you mean?" asked Cally's mom. Cally realized she'd omitted this part of the story in her last night's recounting.

"Shamus and I saw Tanglebell's back up a huge tanker-trailer, rig up a line and literally pump liquid waste-stuff into the stream."

"Anyway," said Cally, turning everyone's attention back to the screen. She showed the goldenrod fanning out on the surface of Foggy Bottom. "We really could trace the fact that the stream goes into the lake. And the oil and whatever else they put into the waste dump and the stream ends up in the lake. See?" Cally pointed to the next image of an oil slick at the edge of the lake. "And look, the fish are dying. And this poor seagull. It couldn't get the oil off its wings. It was covered."

Cally moved the laptop around so everyone could see.

"That's powerful stuff," said Shamus. "I'm going to need a double spread in the paper."

"And don't forget the last couple of pictures," prompted Giles.

Cally clicked forward in the presentation. "Right. So," she paused, thinking how to introduce the last point. "Mom, Aunt Beth, remember when Giles and I kayaked round towards the lighthouse?"

The sisters nodded.

"Well," she continued, "We explored the beach near there and found oil in the rock pools at the bottom of the cliff, and in the water coming down the side of the cliff." She showed the rainbow shimmer of oil in a rockpool. "And yesterday we checked where those pools were, you know, relative to where Foggy Bottom is, by lining up with the lighthouse and a rock. And we found that the oily rock pools are right below Foggy Bottom."

"So, you think on top of all the ground water pollution, it's going into the ocean too?" asked Cally's mom.

"Yep," said Giles. Cally nodded. She noticed that Shamus was scribbling hard in his notebook.

Petra stood back from the screen. "This is SO bad! You guys are the BEST. Beth, Janie, you have to believe it! They've done a huge service to Moms and to me and to Penzance." She glanced back down at the screen. "Wow, is that the time? Shame, we've got to go. We're going to buy gallons of bottled water from the store to set Moms up with before she gets home."

Cally closed the computer, while Giles handed his memory stick to Shamus. "The photos are all on there," he said.

"So, what happens next?" asked Cally's mom.

"I'll write all this up," said Shamus, shaking the memory card in his hand. "And I'm going to make an appointment with someone high up in the Tanglebell organization, to get a statement from them. Their head office is down in New Hampshire," said Shamus. "That's going to be an interesting meeting."

"And I'm going to get the federal government involved," said Petra. "I'll send a letter to the EPA, the Environmental Protection Agency. Someone's got to protect Moms. She can't use bottled water forever. But whatever happens, I'll keep you two up to speed. When do you leave?"

"Tomorrow morning," said Cally.

"Bright and early," added her mom.

"Oh, and one more thing," Shamus said, as he stood up. He turned with a serious look first to Cally's mom and Aunt Beth, "With your parents' permission…" He turned back to Cally and Giles, "I would like you two to be co-authors on the finished article."

"Wow," said Cally and Giles in unison.

"Sure thing," said her mom. "Let's all see a copy of your exposé before it goes to press."

"Of course," said Shamus. "You've got to be proud of these two. They'd make fine investigative reporters."

"OK, so this is goodbye, for now at least," said Petra. "Catch you online?" this to Giles and Cally.

"Sure," said Giles.

"Email me," said Cally. "Soon I'll have my own cell-phone too. Right, mom?"

"Don't push it, miss," smiled her mom. "But yes, your dad agreed it's time."

With the departure of Petra and Shamus, silence descended on the dining room. Giles reached for his crutches while Cally's mom settled the check and Aunt Beth took the computer in preparation to leave. It's now or never, thought Cally.

"Wait a moment," she said. "Can you all sit down again for a minute. I want to tell you what I've been thinking about the Singapore thing."

Her mom looked up from signing and smiled. "Yeah, with all this excitement I forgot to ask. What's the decision?" Beth sat back down in her chair, and Giles took the crutches out from under his armpits.

"Now she tells us!" he said, as he plopped back down with a thump.

"Yep."

All eyes were on Cally. She spread her hands on the table, her thumbs touching. "Well," she said, "it was what Giles said to me that made up my mind."

Giles gave her a questioning look. She smiled back.

"You remember, when we were talking about Singapore, on the beach after the ice creams? You said, I should aim to have fun. That's what your mom told you, you said, in a letter she wrote. And I think that's right. And I think that Singapore would probably be the most fun."

Her mom opened her mouth to speak, a look of pure pleasure on her face. But Cally rushed on...

"And I wanted to suggest something else too. Dad said we'll have a really big house. My idea is this. Why don't

Aunt Beth and Uncle Ernest and Giles come too? I mean Uncle Ernest can write books anywhere, and Aunt Beth," she looked over at her aunt, "couldn't you edit anywhere if you had internet access? And I know Giles thinks that the idea of Singapore would be cool. And we'd all get a year together in the sun."

"Wow," said Giles. He stared at Cally, his eyes wide with surprise. He nodded slowly.

"Now that's what I call an idea." He turned and gave his step-mother a long, hopeful look. Beth returned his gaze.

There's a lot going on here, Cally thought, suddenly doubting the wisdom of her announcement. Should she and her mom leave them to it? Should she have said something to her mom first? Everyone seemed to be holding their breath.

Finally, Beth blinked. "Is that true, Giles?" Her voice caught. "Would you like the three of us to go too?"

"Are you kidding me? Let's see…" He held out his hands, palms up, mimicking weighing something in each hand. "Albany versus Singapore? Singapore versus Albany? No contest. Singapore wins!"

Cally's mother laughed. "It's a great solution, Cally. I should have thought of it myself. What do you think Sis?"

Beth's face was pink. She had tears in her eyes. "I'll

text Ernest," she said and reached into her purse.

"I'll text Doug too." Cally's mom reached for her phone too. "I'm sure he'll say yes."

"He already did," Cally said.

"What?" said her mother.

Cally nodded. "I emailed him last night. He said that he loves the idea and that the house is plenty big enough for all six of us."

"You did? He did?" Her mom sounded incredulous. "And he didn't even mention it to me."

"He said that I should tell you all," said Cally, unable to keep the pride and happiness from her voice.

"Wow," said her mom, momentarily at a loss for words. "That's good, that's right," she said hastily. She turned to her sister. "So, it's up to you and Ernest," she said. "Could we possibly make this work?"

Chapter
19

The last afternoon of the vacation was spent in a strange limbo. Her mom and aunt's first idea had been to spend it on the beach but, as they emerged from the hotel, a cold east wind began to blow. Aunt Beth opened the door for Giles to come through on his crutches.

"I'm not sure this is such a great plan," she said as he emerged. "How will you manage on the sand?"

"I can hop," he said, gamely.

Cally looked at her cousin and thought that her aunt had made a good point. "How about we drive over to the waterfall, instead?" she suggested. "We could get an ice cream?"

With her mom at the wheel of the Subaru and Giles navigating by GPS, they found the road leading to the hidden waterfall and whiled away a happy hour over ice creams and coffee. Cally was pleased that the conversation centered around Singapore. She was relieved not to bring up the subject of Foggy Bottom even once. Before dinner, when there had still been no decision from Giles' dad, Giles and Cally adjourned to his room while the sisters went for one final stroll around the harbor.

Giles was in his usual position stretched out on the kid's comforter on the bed while Cally scrolled the website of the Singapore American Academy on her laptop.

"So that really could be us next year," she said, showing Giles the photos of kids in red shorts and white t-shirts. "Dad said they've got a really cool swimming pool." She scrolled on through the frames to a picture of kids wearing headphones. The text box read *Eighth grade language lab.* "Would you take Chinese?" she asked.

"Not for just one year," said Giles. "Makes no sense. But I don't know. Maybe we shouldn't get our hopes up. He still hasn't called. It's been hours."

"Right. I hope he gets back soon." She turned around in her seat to look at Giles. "Tell me again what he said to Aunt Beth in his text?"

"I told you already." He sounded impatient but he carried on… "He'd got the message, loves the idea, is thinking through the *logistics,* whatever that means."

"How much it costs, I'll bet. Airfares to Singapore can't be cheap." Cally felt her spirits fall. "Do you think he'll say yes?"

"This morning I was certain. I was positive he would.

But the more he thinks about it... I don't know." Giles shook his head. "He doesn't know your mom and dad very well. Maybe that's the problem."

A loud knock at the door made them both look up. "They're back," said Cally. "I'll get it."

"Thanks," said Giles. "Beth doesn't have a keycard."

A vaguely familiar figure met Cally's eyes as she opened the door. She looked into the face of a tall, disheveled middle-aged man with a grey beard. She saw the twinkling green eyes and thought, Giles' dad.

"Cally," he said.

"Uncle Ernest," she said, and flung the door wide.

Giles was off the bed and hopping across the room. He met his father half-way across.

"Dad!" he said as he was enveloped in a bear-hug.

"Hey Giles."

A moment passed. Cally wondered whether she should leave them to their reunion. But there was one big question to be answered before she left. She waited.

"What are you doing here?" Giles asked, as he emerged from his dad's arms.

"Well, let's see." His father stood back and started to enumerate with his thumb and fingers. He had a pleasant, sing-song voice. "Missed you, that's one; missed Beth, that's two. Three, I'm suffering from writer's block. Then four, I wanted to see the ocean, and five, I thought it might help to have the jeep to drive home in since you've hurt your ankle." He paused, held up his other hand and then let it drop. "But more than anything else, I wanted to join in the planning for next year. So, I got in the car and I drove. Five and a half hours exactly," he said. He scanned the room and threw down an over-night bag on the bed. "Is there room in here for me tonight?"

Giles did not appear to hear the last question. "Next year?" he asked.

Cally held her breath.

"Yes. I hear that we're all going to Singapore."

"Yes," she breathed.

"Yeahh!" Giles shouted. He turned to her, hand held high. "High five, fellow adventurer," he said.

Their hands slapped together as their eyes met. The air reverberated around them.

"Singapore, here we come!" Cally said.

Cally left Giles to chat with his dad and went in search of her mom and aunt. They must be finished with their walk by now, she thought, since it was already dark outside. Cally guessed that they had to have been in on Uncle Ernest's surprise trip. She'd wager a bet that they had known about it, all the time that they'd been chatting in Mollie's. They'd known that he'd been in his car driving from Albany to Maine. Grown-ups can keep secrets too, she thought. She smiled to herself. It had been so good to see Giles' expression when he first saw his dad. He'd looked like all his Christmases had come at once.

This vacation really has involved sun and sand and sea and ice cream and rock pools and splashing in the waves, she thought, as she walked back to her room. But also much more. She rounded the turn in the corridor and caught sight of the two sisters as they strolled along ahead of her. Cally ran the few yards into the space between them and caught hold of their hands.

"So, I've just seen Uncle Ernest," she said. "You knew, didn't you? Next year we're going to be one BIG happy family!"

This story evolved. It would never have been published without the advice of the writer and teacher of writing, Margaret Meacham. It would never have had depth without the influence of my daughter, Sara and it will never get read unless you, the reader enjoys it and hands it on.

— Janet Wylie

Janet Wylie is a retired professor of developmental biology, who had the joy of studying embryonic development for a living at the same time as helping her children grow up. Now she is a novice writer of fiction for middle school readers, buoyed by the help and enthusiasm of other writers. She hopes to entertain in two ways: first by providing a good read, an adventure in a vacation location scarred by pollution, and second by exploring the real world of emotions and decision-making that confronts kids faced with environmental and personal challenges.

bsite: janetwyliewords.com